the noah confessions

the noah confessions

BARBARA HALL

Delacorte Press

ACKNOWLEDGMENTS

Thanks to Beverly Horowitz for coaxing the story out of me with the right amount of persuasion, encouragement, and deadline. Thanks to Rebecca Gudelis for keeping the time-line monster in his cage and dressed for dinner. Thanks to my agent, Cynthia Manson, for her tireless enthusiasm, to the W.F.'s for putting up with the disappearing act, Dave Marsh for the porch I almost used, and my sister, Karen, for always getting it.

Published by Delacorte Press
an imprint of Random House Children's Books
a division of Random House, Inc., New York

www.randomhouse.com/teens
Educators and librarians, for a variety of teaching tools,
visit us at www.randomhouse.com/teachers

Library of Congress Cataloging-in-Publication Data
Hall, Barbara.
The Noah confessions / Barbara Hall. — 1st ed.
p. cm.
Summary: Instead of a car for her sixteenth birthday, Lynnie receives from her father a manuscript in which her deceased mother writes about family secrets, helping Lynnie to understand more about her parents and the complexity of growing up.
ISBN: 978-0-385-73328-1 (trade)   ISBN: 978-0-385-90346-2 (lib. bdg.)
[1. Family problems—Fiction.   2. Fathers and daughters—Fiction.
3. Mothers—Fiction.]   I. Title.
PZ7.H1407No 2007   [Fic]—dc22   2006015640

The text of this book is set in 11.5-point Berkeley Oldstyle.
Printed in the United States of America
10 9 8 7 6 5 4 3 2 1
First Edition

For Faith

MOM'S SIDE
(starting in Virginia)

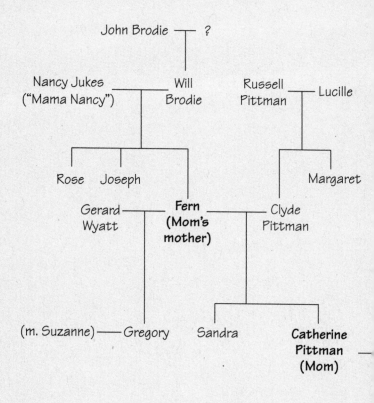

John Brodie — ?

Nancy Jukes ("Mama Nancy") — Will Brodie

Russell Pittman — Lucille

Rose Joseph

Margaret

Gerard Wyatt — **Fern (Mom's mother)** — Clyde Pittman

(m. Suzanne) — Gregory

Sandra

Catherine Pittman (Mom)

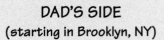

DAD'S SIDE
(starting in Brooklyn, NY)

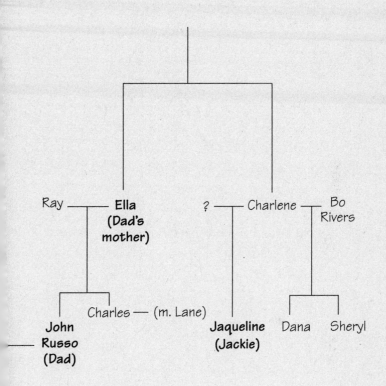

Ray ——— Ella
(Dad's
mother)

? ——— Charlene ——— Bo
Rivers

Charles — (m. Lane)

John
Russo
(Dad)

Jaqueline
(Jackie)

Dana   Sheryl

**What I've figured out about my family
by me, Jacqueline Julia "Lynnie" Russo**

SIXTEEN

• 1 •

It was my sixteenth birthday and my father wouldn't buy me a car.

This was all the talk at Hillsboro, the fancy girls' prep school I attended in Los Angeles, which we all pretended to hate but secretly adored.

I thought he had been teasing me all this time. He used to do that when I was little, telling me the Powers that Be had canceled Christmas or moved Disneyland. I never believed him. It just made me laugh. So I thought it was part of the routine when he kept saying, "I'm serious, Lynnie, no car."

"Right, Dad."

"This is for real."

"I get it."

Obviously, I didn't get it.

When I woke up that day and tore into the jewelry box sitting in the empty cereal bowl, I didn't find a gleaming Volkswagen key. I found a dull silver charm bracelet with birds on it.

You read that right. A charm bracelet. With birds on it.

My father, who was not a stupid man, smiled and waited. I just stared at him with my jaw unhinged.

"It's a charm bracelet," he said.

"Yeah, with birds on it."

He said, "It's vintage."

"Right."

"Do you like it?"

"Dad, come on, where's the real present?"

His face deflated and I felt horrible and horrified at the same time.

"I told you. There is no car."

"You were serious?"

"I told you."

"But why?"

"Because you don't need a car. You barely know how to drive."

"That's not the point."

He sat down next to me and held the bird bracelet up.

"Sweetie, this belonged to your mother."

That didn't have the effect he was hoping for. I already had a lot of my mother's jewelry, all of it nicer than this.

But he had that look on his face that he got whenever my mother came up. I couldn't torture him, no matter how mad I was. I just kissed him and took the bracelet and went upstairs to dress. I put it on because I didn't want to hurt his feelings, but it was all kinds of ugly. First, it didn't appear to be real silver. More like nickel. And the birds were deformed-looking, some of them with their wings and beaks chipped off. It wasn't close to something I'd ever wear. It wasn't even something my mother would wear.

The whole ordeal felt like a punishment. I hadn't done anything wrong except turn sixteen. And he couldn't be mad at me about that.

The ride to school that day was quiet. As we cruised along the Pacific Coast Highway, I glanced at the ocean and the surfers bobbing in the waves. I wondered what they were thinking. Then I remembered that surfers mostly didn't think. So I wondered what they were feeling, hurling themselves into the arctic water before breakfast.

I'd always wanted to try it. Normally I'd say a thing like that out loud to my father, but today I was quiet.

As we merged onto the 10 freeway, my father said, "Gee, feels like you could hang meat in here."

"Oh, did you say something? I couldn't hear you over the sound of my heart smashing into pieces."

"Sweetie, the thing about the car, it's complicated."

I had no response to that.

"And I thought you'd like the bracelet."

I twisted it on my wrist and felt the birds poking into my skin.

I always understood that I might not get a *new* car, because he thought that was showy and spoiled and I didn't disagree. In fact, I was relishing the idea of being the pragmatic, environmentally sensitive, politically correct girl. I had speeches prepared about my used VW Beetle. "You know, even the hybrid SUVs burn more fossil fuels than my car, and they break down more often, which is bad for the environment." I had no idea if this was true.

This wasn't about showing off. All the girls in my circle pretended *not* to be rich. It wasn't cool to be rich. We tried to act middle class and socially responsible. We worried about people in Somalia and women in burkas and the disappearing rain forests, and we hated Humvees and we thought everyone should be eating a third less meat. The only area where we were willing to exhibit some rampant consumerism was in the area of the car. You got one on your sixteenth birthday. You just did.

Except me. I just didn't.

As we approached the school I said, "Any idea of what I should say to people? I mean, you never fully explained it."

"Tell them we're not from here."

"But I am from here."

"Then tell them I'm not. I do things differently. Blame it on your horrible, mean, miserly father and his cracker background."

I didn't know how to break it to him that this approach would not fly. We were all from L.A., regardless of where our parents grew up, and if there was anything resembling a connection to another place, unless it was Europe, we all denied it. The fact that my parents grew up somewhere in the swamps of the South, where no one speaks correctly, let alone knows how to vote, well, that just was not going to come up over our lunches of seaweed and brown rice on the finely manicured lawn of Hillsboro.

Besides, the fact that he was not from here was a totally lame excuse. He was a lawyer, which was embarrassing, but he was an ACLU lawyer before he went into private practice, which meant he spent a respectable amount of time worried about the poor, the disenfranchised, issues of diversity, and so on. Every year they called on him to present the civics award. I always blushed when he stood up to make the speech. But when he started talking I relaxed, because his voice had a silvery quality and he looked like a middle-aged rock star. You would be able to glance at him in a mall or a grocery store and say, "That guy was once cool."

So the car ordeal didn't make sense. Except it did. In a way that we could not discuss.

We pulled up in front of the school, behind the cars of eighth and ninth graders being driven by their parents. Upper-classmen were parking their cars across the street, in the lot that required a special decal.

"I really don't see why this is such a big deal," he said as I got out, dragging my backpack.

I held my tongue hard. I had never said it to him in all this time, in eight years, no matter how tempted I had been, I hadn't said it and I didn't want to start now.

"Bye, Dad." I slammed the door.

Mom would have understood. That's what I didn't say.

• 2 •

Zoe and Talia were my best friends. Zoe was short and cute with curly hair and she never stopped talking. Talia was beautiful with a great sense of style and a heightened sense of drama. They were waiting for me at my locker, which was decorated with streamers and pom-poms and candy. Part of the tradition on your sixteenth was taping up a picture of your car.

Zoe hugged me. "Finally, finally. Our baby is growing up."

"Funny, Mom."

This was a reference to me being the youngest in the class by a year, the result of a nursery school teacher who had declared me a genius and encouraged my parents to skip me a grade. Later they found out that she had bipolar disorder and she was sent away to recover, but I still carried the legacy of that chance encounter.

Talia got right to the point. "Is it a Beetle?"

"No, it's a charm bracelet."

"What?"

I held up my wrist.

"Are those birds?"

"Yes, they are birds. You get to go to the bonus round."

"But you're getting a car, too," Zoe said.

"Nope."

She had a white Honda and Talia had a blue Mini. They had given their cars names. The Honda was called Stephanie and the Mini was called Fernando. My Beetle was going to be D. J. Dynasty Handbag, after a character on *SNL*. D.J. for short.

"That is bizarre, truly," Talia said, sinking her teeth into the drama. "There must be a reason. Some dark, twisted reason."

"It's because he's not from here. Because he's from the South and he grew up poor and he didn't get a car: That's what he says. But I know it's because of my mother."

"What about your mother?" Talia went wide-eyed. "You mean other than she's dead?"

"Yeah, I can't come up with anything bigger than that."

"Oh, right, and she died in a car."

In a bad car wreck. Everyone phrased it that way. "A bad car wreck, when Lynnie was little." As if there were such a thing as a good car wreck. Exactly fifteen minutes after dropping me off at school on a Tuesday morning when I was in the third grade. Drunk driver. Bad drunk driver.

My father came to pick me up from school. I still remembered his face in the rectangular window outside my classroom. The teacher led me to the hall. My father knelt down to be at eye level with me. He said, "Lynnie, Mommy is gone." It was that simple. And part of me still blamed him just because he was the one who said it. I remember going very still and thinking, Don't cry, don't show anything. Because if you show something it will be real, not just for you but for him. I started taking care of him right that moment.

And I hadn't stopped. I didn't know how to stop. Which was why I was wearing the stupid bird bracelet and why I hadn't cried or complained as much as I wanted to about the car. I had to let it go. He had been through enough and I was all he had.

How did I know this? I knew it because he didn't have a life outside of me. He just worked and came home. He never dated. Sometimes he still watched videos from when Mom was alive, and he always had a Scotch at night, but that could have been a lawyer thing.

But it honestly hadn't occurred to me until that very moment that he was trying to protect me from the same fate. How could I not have seen it? How could it have fallen on Talia's sense of tragedy to bring it into focus?

"Bad car wreck," I said. I could feel the blood rushing to my face and I didn't know if I was mad or embarrassed or some emotion I couldn't identify.

"Eight years ago," Zoe said quietly. I looked at her. It was the voice of reason coming out of the wilderness. "That was eight years ago. I mean, geez."

"Way to be sensitive," Talia said. "As if you ever get over a thing like that."

Zoe shrugged. "But he lets you ride with other people. *He* drives a car."

I shook my head. "That's different."

The noises in the hall seemed very loud and I felt light-headed.

"Lynne, are you okay?" Zoe asked.

"Yeah, you look all white," Talia said.

"Maybe I need air."

"We're outside."

"Maybe I need different air. I'll see you guys later. I have to get to homeroom," I said. "History . . ."

I walked away in a haze of understanding.

• 3 •

Jen Connor was sitting under a tree, ignoring everyone and being ignored, flipping through a magazine. I didn't know her well. At Hillsboro she was considered an underachiever, one of those rare girls who didn't care about her grades or if she got into any college, let alone an Ivy League. She was a surf bum. One of those people who made it look as if surfers never thought about anything but water and wind.

My father and I lived in the Palisades, in the hills staring down at the ocean, and I could see them floating out there like sea mammals. When my mother was alive she would take me for walks on the beach and we'd stop and sit on the sand and watch them catching waves. She rooted for them and clapped and yelled, which embarrassed me even then, but my mother had great and noisy enthusiasm for things.

"If I were younger I'd try it," she'd say.

I didn't think it had to do with being younger, though. It had to do with this strange sense of longing and sadness my mother had, as if she'd missed out on something, as if there were a party she had not been invited to.

I remembered her reading "Cinderella" to me when I was little and I asked her why the stepmother was so mean and why the father didn't come home and she said, "Oh, sweetie, sometimes people just lose their way in the world."

I wasn't any expert in child psychology, but it seemed like a complicated answer to a simple question. I would have been happy with "It's just a story."

"Hey, Lizard," Jen said without looking up. She gave me that nickname last year when we were science lab partners. I had already forgotten why. I just remembered I had done all the work.

"Hey, Jen."

"Happy birthday. I saw your locker."

"Thanks."

"What are you, seventeen?"

"Sixteen. I skipped a grade."

"What'd you get?"

I held up my wrist.

She squinted at the bracelet and said, "I mean, the ride."

"Didn't get one," I said. "My dad has a hangup about driving."

She stuck out her lip and nodded as if this were vaguely interesting.

"What did you get?" I asked.

"My birthday was last March. I got a Toyota truck. Throw my boards in the back. You know."

"Yeah."

I hesitated, swaying on my feet.

"So I was thinking. Since it's my birthday and I feel like doing something crazy, would you teach me how to surf?"

"That is so random," she said.

"Are you going out today?"

"Yeah, I'll probably hit Sunset. If you want to go."

"I do."

She laughed, tossing her sun-bleached hair over her shoulder.

"Dude," she said, "way to get your father back. If he won't let you drive, I gotta think he hates you surfing."

"Yeah," I said. "That occurred to me."

She closed her magazine and glanced at the big diving watch she wore on her tanned arm.

"No time like the present," she said.

I laughed nervously. "What do you mean? We're a minute away from first bell."

She cocked her head at me and said, "Do you feel sick? You look sick to me."

"No, I'm not sick. Wait. What are you suggesting?"

First bell sounded and she stuffed her magazine into her backpack.

"Meet me in the parking lot. We never had this conversation, of course."

She stood up and walked away.

I stood in the quad and felt all the students rushing past me, running to their homerooms, and there was a very strong pull to be where I was supposed to be. But the birds were dancing against my arm, and I could barely hear my mother's voice anymore, and I knew I had to do something different. It was my birthday, after all, and if I wasn't getting a car, I needed to do something outrageous, something to prove that it wasn't me who had died in the bad car wreck.

I ran to my decorated locker and stuffed my belongings into it. Then I glanced around to see who was watching. No one was. I walked calmly away from the front of the school, crossed the street, and found myself in the upperclassmen parking lot, surrounded by all those cars that were not mine.

Jen was leaning against her black pickup truck, her board jutting out like a natural appendage. She raised her chin when she saw me approaching.

"You're saving me," she said. "I was totally unprepared for my geometry quiz."

"You'll get an incomplete," I said with a sense of alarm I should have disguised.

She laughed. "I learn more about math in the water than I do in class. Climb in."

I got into her truck and she turned up the tunes and I felt all loose and crazy, as if we were on our way to rob a bank or make some other misstep from which I'd never recover. I thought of my father in his office, assuming everything was right with the world. I never defied him this way. I felt the sweat breaking out on my forehead but I was too embarrassed to tell Jen.

We pulled out of the parking lot and she said, "Anywhere you want to go before we hit the water? We could get subs or something."

"It's barely eight o'clock."

"Yeah, time is not such an important thing in my world."

She turned up the volume and drummed the dash.

I thought, Wow, there's a whole world where the accepted structure just doesn't matter. Getting good grades, playing by the rules, pleasing people, none of it mattered. I wondered what did matter in a universe like that, but I didn't feel brave enough to ask.

"Well," I said, "since we're on the road, there's somewhere I want to go."

"Yeah? Name it."

"Westwood," I said.

"Westwood? What's there besides movie theaters and chain restaurants and creepy UCLA students?"

"There's a cemetery," I said. I was about to elaborate but I didn't need to. She got it. After all, I was one of the few kids at Hillsboro with a dead mother.

"Sure, I'll take you there," she said. "But don't get all morose. We'll stop off. But the point is, we're surfing."

"I'm down with it," I said, feeling automatically embarrassed. She didn't have a big response to my outdated vernacular. Either she wasn't listening or I just didn't register on her radar.

Jen parked the truck on a side street, right behind the cemetery. It was hidden away behind a Presbyterian church on Wilshire Boulevard, and most people didn't know about it. A few film buffs knew it existed because Marilyn Monroe was buried there. Occasionally you'd see tourists in clumps with their cameras, but mostly it was empty and serene. It was completely devoid of people this time of day. I walked past various graves and Jen lagged behind. I glanced back and saw that she had lit a cigarette and was staring at the clouds. I didn't know what I was doing with her. I didn't know what I was doing at all.

As we approached the grave markers, she suddenly stopped and called out to me.

"Hey, I'm parked in a red zone," she said. "I'll hang by the truck, but don't be too long."

I watched her heading back to the street. Her profile looked cool and sophisticated. But she was afraid of the cemetery.

I found my mother's grave without trying. I visited it frequently, sometimes with my father but most times without. It was a small gravestone, off-white marble, and it said nothing more than this: Catherine Russo. Beloved wife and mother. May she rest with God. 1960–1997. I had stared at that headstone a number of times, trying to recall something of my mother while standing in front of her grave. It was still hard for me. She was in the kitchen, making cookies, or she was in my bedroom, singing me to sleep. Dead was a thing I still could not imagine her being. They hadn't let me see her in the coffin. I was too little. Sometimes I tried to imagine it, but the scene always looked like it did on TV, an alive person trying not to breathe.

The message on the stone seemed phony. Even though we talked about God, we never went to church, and nobody could be sure my mother was resting with God.

I felt it should say, "Bad Car Wreck, Bad Drunk Driver."

"Okay," I said to the stone, "here I am on my sixteenth birthday and Dad won't buy me a car because you died in one, so I'm doing this unpredictable thing that I know is bad but I have to do it and you'll just have to understand."

I heard the edge in my voice and for the first time I realized I might be mad at her, too, for dying, for not leaving better

13

instructions, for not telling my father how to raise me. I was sure she'd planned on being around. But she wasn't. And no one had told him how to be a mother.

"If you are where they say you are, and if you have any magical powers there, could you please help change his mind? Dad, that is. About the car. It would mean a lot to me."

There was no answer.

I glanced up and looked around, and I didn't see anything but a boy about my age sitting nearby, under a tree, drawing in a sketchbook. Our eyes connected and he smiled and I wanted to smile back. His hair was long and too much in his eyes, and it had been years since rocking the army jacket was in style. I thought about saying something. Our looks converged and our expressions stalled and I wanted to walk right up to him. I wanted to say, "Hey, you skip school? I skip school, too."

But he dismissed me and looked back down at his drawing. He could tell I didn't skip school. I wasn't really a bad girl.

I turned back to the stone.

"Thanks for the bracelet, Mom. I have to tell you, it's kind of ugmo. But I'll wear it because it's yours. I miss you."

"Are we done here?"

This was Jen's voice from a distance. She was pointing at her watch.

I walked to meet her, glancing just once to see what the boy was doing. He was drawing.

"Yelling in a graveyard," I said to Jen. "Now, that's classy."

She said, "Dude, enough with the dead people. Let's hit the waves."

• 4 •

She parked the truck in an open parking lot near the beach. She had extra gear, including an extra board and a wet suit, which she taught me how to put on. It was like climbing back into the womb, but as soon as I had it on, I felt official, as if I would automatically know how to surf.

She put her hand up like a shield against the sun and watched the waves.

"It's closing out fast, but the wave itself is slow. You can learn on this."

She jumped on her board and started paddling into the waves. I climbed on mine and it squeaked and squirreled under my body. It was all I could do to stay on top, and every time I paddled, a wave would come and push me off. The board would shoot out and I would go chasing it like a dog after a giant Frisbee. This went on for a while and I could hear Jen laughing beyond the break.

"Lizard," she called out, "just arch up and the wave will go under you."

So I tried it and she was right. The board lifted right up like a little boat and the white water sprayed my face, but I stayed on. A few more of those and I was right next to Jen, where the water was calm, right before the waves re-formed. We had a minute to rest and she spoke quickly.

She said, "You'll hear the wave before you feel it. Look back to make sure it's a good size. Then paddle as hard as you can.

As soon as you get a ride, arch up, then stand up, and let the wave do the rest. Watch first."

I let the next wave wash over me but she caught it, and I watched as she jumped up and rode it like a magic carpet all the way to the shore. It looked easy and natural, but when I tried to imitate her I found myself barely able to stand. When I did, the nose of the board went down and then I was in the spin cycle and I had sand in my mouth. I came up spitting and Jen was paddling by me and she just said, "Stand farther back on the board."

We spent most of the day like that, her sailing in like a pro and me blowing the move in some humorous or painful way. Once I rode in to the shore on my knees. That gave me an idea of how great it was going to be when I finally made it. But on the next two tries I missed the waves altogether and I was starting to get exhausted.

Jen paddled up next to me and straddled her board. I was taking a breather. I was cold and I was starting to feel guilty and the surfer's high had not hit me yet.

"You're just scared, Lizard," she told me.

"Oh, is that all it is?"

"Yeah, the ocean freaks people out. It's too real."

"It's also loud and mean."

"It's none of those things. It's just in charge. Soon as you realize that, you'll be fine."

"Great," I said. "Yet another way to feel powerless."

"Why did you want to learn this? Was it really to piss your dad off?"

"I don't know. I think I wanted something that could be

mine. That didn't have to do with my mother or him or school or the future. Just a moment in time when I get it, you know?"

"You'll get it. It's called the click. One minute, it all just makes sense."

"I wish I could find the click in life."

"You, me, and everybody. Come on, last set. Just let go and ride."

The last wave lifted me up and I felt empowered and I scrambled to my feet. For a few seconds I was walking on water. I stood tall and saw the shore rushing toward me and felt the rest of the ocean fading behind me, and I was completely suspended in time and space. It didn't last long. I fell off into the restless water and it churned me around. When I came up spitting, Jen was grinning at me.

"That's how it's done," she said.

She drove me home and we were both quiet from exhaustion. I was feeling mildly euphoric. I had surfed. I was going to surf. I was a surfer. And I wasn't feeling stupid at all. I still had room to think about things. I could see my new life, my own special persona unfolding across the horizon like the ocean itself.

It wasn't until we pulled up in my driveway and I saw my dad's car that reality showed up like an obnoxious guest.

"What's he going to do?" she asked.

"I don't know. He can't kill me. Anyway, it was worth it."

She smiled and gave me some kind of surfing hand gesture that I didn't attempt to return. I didn't need to fake it anymore.

I turned and the bubble of euphoria burst.

My father's face was at the door and the birds were digging into my wrist.

• 5 •

He was still in his work clothes and his arms were crossed. He hadn't even touched his glass of Scotch. He was too busy staring. His ears were red.

"Who the hell do you think you are?" he asked.

"That's not a real question."

His ears went redder. "Oh, you want a statement? You're grounded until college."

"You knew I was upset."

"So that's an appropriate response to being disappointed in your birthday present?"

"It's not just a present. It's a milestone and I missed it. I had to do something for the occasion."

"Yes, I don't think you're going to forget this occasion. Ms. Gardner called. You got two demerits. Another one and you're suspended."

"I won't get another one. I'm the good kid. I never get in trouble. Remember?"

He stared at me and his breathing started to slow. He took a sip of Scotch. My hair was dripping on the rug. I sucked the salt water out of the ends.

"What did you do? Go swimming?"

"Surfing," I said.

"Surfing."

"Yes, and I got up, which is rare your first time, and I think I might actually be good at it."

"Surfing. By yourself."

"With a friend."

"With a friend and the undertow and the riptides and the sharks."

"Dad, seriously. Life isn't safe. You can't lock me up."

"I'm not saying that."

"But it's why you didn't get me a car."

He took another sip of Scotch. "Is that what you think?"

"Well, isn't it?"

"No, in fact, it isn't."

"Then tell me what it's about."

"I'm not sure you're ready."

"I'm two years from being an adult. Don't you have a clue? Dad, I love you, but a charm bracelet with birds on it? Really."

He said, "You just don't know what that bracelet means."

"Then why don't you tell me?"

"It's important," he said.

"So tell me."

Another hit of Scotch and the glass was empty.

"You want to know? Even if it changes your whole perspective?"

"Yes."

He stared at me for a long time. Then he turned and climbed the stairs and went into his room. I heard him moving around the room for a while and then he came back, carrying a manuscript box. He dropped it on the table and gestured for me to sit down. I did.

He leaned over the box and touched its corners. He stared at it for a long time and when he spoke his voice was softer.

"Lynnie, your childhood is so much different from mine."

"I know."

"No, you really don't."

It was true. I had never asked. I knew they were both from the South. I knew they had met in high school and then again in Los Angeles. I knew I had never seen any of my relatives. Whenever I asked why, they were vague. There had been a misunderstanding. Hard feelings. Grudges. I assumed everyone had disapproved of the marriage and that was where I left it. You don't miss relatives if you've never had them. It's like missing a place you've never visited.

I knew there would come a time when I was curious about my ancestors, but this wasn't it.

"You have a great life, whether you know it or not. Even with losing your mother. You have me, you have friends, you have interests, you have school, and most of all, you have a future. You're going to college. You'll pursue your dreams. Nothing is going to hinder that if I can help it."

I opened my mouth to respond but he raised a finger.

"I know you think that's true of everyone, but it isn't. Sometimes people are born into problems they didn't create. Bigger problems than not having a car."

"Dad, I got an A in Global Studies."

He shook his head. "This is different."

He stared at the box for a moment, as if it contained gold or dynamite, and then he pushed it toward me.

"Your mother and I discussed this moment. We decided it was for when you were mature enough. Or for when you started to lose perspective. I think both of those things are happening now."

I took the box and lifted it. It was heavy. Nothing moved inside. It didn't make a noise.

"Open it," he said.

I lifted the top.

Inside I saw a bulging manila envelope. It was taped shut and nothing was written on it.

"Something you wrote?" I asked.

He shook his head. "No, not me."

I opened the envelope and took out the manuscript. It was typewritten and neatly stacked, though the edges were frayed and yellow.

It was at least a hundred pages, bound by brass brads.

I glanced at the first page. It said: "September 25, 1975."

"My birthday," I pointed out.

"A coincidence," he said, "if you believe in that kind of thing."

Dear Noah,

Please allow me to introduce myself. I'm a girl of wealth and taste.

I ripped that off from a song. Ten points if you know which one.

"That's the Rolling Stones," I said. "'Sympathy for the Devil.'"

He nodded.

I saw you for the first time today when Ms. McKeever introduced you in English class. My name is Catherine Pittman. Call me Cat because everyone does.

I looked at him.

"That's Mom."

"Yes."

"But who's Noah?"

"He's the guy who built the ark."

"No, Dad, really."

"Just read it."

"Does Noah realize you have this letter?"

"He knows."

I looked back down at it. I had that creepy feeling you get when looking at old photographs or relics someone dug up in Egypt. All that time had passed but once it had been a shiny new idea.

I felt nervous. I felt the way I had, earlier with Jen, when I missed a good wave and I was alone in the water and the other waves were going to tumble down on top of me. Here was the voice of my mother, the same age as I was now, sitting in my lap, waiting to tell me something.

"This is too much. I can't read it in one night."

"Just get started."

My father kissed me on top of my head.

"Is this a punishment?" I asked him.

"No, Lynnie. This is your gift." Then he left me alone with it.

• 6 •

I took the manuscript up to my room. I put it on one side of the bed and tried to ignore it. I went online and got my homework assignments. Then I put on my iPod and started to get to work.

But the manuscript just sat there beside me, quiet and demanding, like a cat, angling for my attention.

I turned off my iPod and pushed my books to the floor and picked it up.

"Okay, here goes. Happy birthday to me."

I began to read my mother's voice.

It's 1975 and there's an oil shortage and a recession and everyone is really bored with it. Music is pretty good—at least we have the Stones and the Who and Bruce Springsteen and Eric Clapton and there's always Motown. I wonder if you like any of this stuff or if you're some kind of Yes or Jethro Tull freak. We'd talk about all that if we ever got to meet, but I don't think we will.

There are rumors about why your family has moved here. Your father's CIA or FBI and is only pretending to be a dentist because that's his cover. I mean, if you're a dentist and you could live anywhere, wouldn't you want to live somewhere decent? Union Grade, Virginia, is as far as you can get from anything decent. There are less than two thousand people here and way less than half of them are our age and way less than half of those are interesting.

I know the real reason you're here. That's why I'm writing to you.

I know the real reason because I'm a little bit psychic. Don't laugh. Since I was little, I could hear people's thoughts and feel their feelings. It's not some strange cosmic gift. It's just that in my family, I've had to learn how to read and interpret things other than words and smiles.

There is so much going on beneath the surface. I'm what you'd call vigilant.

The more acceptable reason is that I know how to listen to gossip. I hear all the weird stuff and I reject it. I hear the real reason and it just hits home—I know it's true.

Your mother grew up here and she came back to settle some unfinished business. That's what people are saying and they're right. What you'll be surprised to learn is that I'm part of that unfinished business.

I can't go into that right now. First, some history. Mine.

I'm the youngest of three kids. My brother's a Methodist minister in North Carolina. He's married, no kids. My sister is a freshman at William and Mary, majoring in theater. My mother's a housewife. My father runs the carpet factory here in Union Grade. It's the main industry aside from the tire plant and the building supply. He doesn't own it—it's a big corporate monolith based in Tennessee. But he's the manager and that makes him the big man in town. He employs a lot of people, parents of a lot of kids who go to school with us. He's also on the town council and in the Lions Club, and is a deacon in the Methodist church, which we attend regularly.

Are you still awake? Keep going.

The reason I'm writing to you is that I have something to confess.

That's why it's important that we don't get to know each other. As soon as you read this letter it's going to change your life. It's going to change mine. It's way far better if we are strangers when it happens.

What I want to tell you is that I'm a criminal.

No, it's not shoplifting or speeding or taking drugs or buying and selling tests or bootleg records. It's a lot more serious. They send you to prison until you're old or dead.

You're the first person I've ever told and probably the last, unless I decide to go ahead and tell the police and do my time. I'm still thinking of running away. I don't know how it's going to work. I don't know what's going to happen to me if I go through with this. But I have a pretty good idea of what will happen if I don't.

I put the manuscript in the box, the top on the box, and the box under my bed. I walked down the hall to my father's bedroom and didn't even knock. He was sitting in his chair next to the fireplace and had just opened one of his precious books about the Civil War or the trade union movement. He didn't even look up at me.

I said, "Let me get this straight. This is a letter from my mother to some boy named Noah, when she was sixteen, wherein she confesses to said strange boy named after the guy in the ark that she's a criminal?"

My father looked to the ceiling. "I think she was fifteen."

"Hilarious. You see my sides splitting."

"Just keep reading, Lynne. Rome wasn't built in a day."

"It's going to take me a hundred typewritten pages to figure out how my mother became a criminal? You're not just going to explain it to me? You don't think it's worth getting right to the point?"

"There's no way to do that," he said. "If I thought . . . If she thought . . . there were another way, she'd have chosen it."

I waited but he just stared at me.

"Congratulations," I said. "I've forgotten about the car."

SIXTEEN
and a Day

• 1 •

I didn't read any more that night. I had a history test the next day and since I had spent most of the first part of the year obsessing about Ms. Kintner's wardrobe (she dressed like Heidi some days, a gypsy or a Portuguese widow on others, and I liked to take bets), I was naturally worried about how I was going to do. Technically I was already grounded until college, even though I was pretty sure my father was using hyperbole to prove a point. Still, I didn't want to throw bad grades into the mix. I studied as much as possible but it wasn't easy, not with the letter sitting under my bed like a bomb.

I didn't sleep much. I tossed and turned and dreamed of waves one minute and guns the next. I saw my mother robbing a bank. I saw myself walking on water. I saw the car that I didn't get going over the side of a cliff with me in it. Then my mother. Then Ms. Kintner. It was an exhausting night and I was relieved when it ended.

My father and I didn't talk about it on the way to school. All he said was "You aren't going to do anything crazy today, are you?"

"If I do, I'll call you."

"Lynnie."

"Don't worry."

But I knew he would.

Everyone was talking about me ditching school. At lunch, younger classmen were pointing and whispering. That's what it was like at Hillsboro. Being a little bad made you a celebrity. Anything more got you kicked out.

"You are so my hero," Talia said.

"Don't be ridiculous, she could end up in public school," Zoe said.

"Her father would never let that happen."

"He went to public school," I said.

"Yeah, but he won't even let you drive a car."

"What did he do to you?" Zoe asked.

"He gave me a letter," I said.

"Oh, that's the worst. Like you want to hear them going on about right and wrong and what happened in their day. I have to go to computer lab."

"Me too," Talia said, and they hurried off, still munching on their veggie wraps.

I watched them go and felt like my whole place in the world was leaking away.

I pictured my mother sitting in a cafeteria in a bad public school in the South, writing in her notebook. I wondered if Noah had been near her, if she could see him across the room, if he was cute, if he knew who she was. I wondered about her crime, how soon I would know and if it would change me. Or my feelings for her.

I saw Jen sitting alone in her usual spot. She had her eyes

28

fixed on a surfing magazine while she ate a slice of pizza, folded in half the way a New Yorker does it.

I kicked the grass in front of her to get her attention. She just looked at my shoes and recognized them.

"Hey, Lizard. You did good yesterday. But I can't skip any more for a while. I nearly got caught."

"I did get caught."

"You'll get better at it."

I sat on the ground and said, "Guess what I got for my birthday?"

"I think we went over this. A bracelet. No car. You need to move on."

"Something else. A letter from my mother."

"From your dead mother?"

"She wrote it when she was fifteen."

"To you?"

"Jen, a little circulation in the brain, if it's not too much trouble."

"You're telling the story," she said. "I can't help that it's all screwed up."

"She wrote it to somebody else when she was about my age."

"Who?"

"A guy named Noah."

"Is it a love letter?"

"No, it's a . . . confession."

"What'd she do?"

"I haven't gotten to that part."

"It's probably boring. Our parents thought they did all this rad shit but it was totally lame. Marijuana. Oooh. I'm scared."

"You don't do drugs."

"Don't need to. I surf. That's my point. Smoking a joint makes you lose your ambition, my father says. I'm like, okay, the wrong break at the wrong time, you're toast."

"Don't scare me. I'm just getting started."

"I'm just saying."

"Can I really read this letter? I mean, do I want to know what she's going to confess?"

Jen pointed to a page in the magazine and said, "Look at that red and yellow Hobie. Sweet."

"Well, thanks for listening."

"Everybody's got a past. You're just trying to keep your mom perfect," she said. "You have that option because she's dead."

This was hands down the smartest thing I'd ever heard her say.

"So you think I should read it."

"Look at it this way, Lizard. Moms are supposed to drive you crazy around this age. Why should yours be different?"

I didn't have an answer.

"Wanna hit Sunset around four o'clock?" she asked. "It should glass out around then, this time of year."

"No, not today."

I wanted to go home and read.

• 2 •

I caught the early bus after school. My dad was at work. The house was still and quiet. I stood at the window and looked at the ocean and thought about Jen being out there and about my future in surfing and how I wished I were just a girl whose biggest problem was that she didn't get a car. But the box was waiting under my bed.

I looked at a picture of my mother that I kept on my desk. She was frozen in that smile I remembered so well, the face that was full of fun ideas and soothing words and whatever I needed in the moment. Until it wasn't there anymore.

But at least it had been frozen in perfection. How could I begin to change that? Why would my father ask me to?

I pulled down the shades and put on my iPod and then I picked up the manuscript.

To look at me, as you almost never do, you would say that I'm a reasonably, even boringly normal person. Long brown hair, parted down the middle, just like all the girls in *Seventeen* magazine. Levi's and T-shirts or sweatshirts identifying some band or food product, a nice sweater on a dress-up day, a skirt when all the girls get together and plan it (we never dress up unless we all agree on it—just like we never go to the bathroom alone). Lip gloss, earrings, knit hats or turquoise belts when I'm feeling fancy. I don't drink or smoke. I get good grades and I belong to the Beta Club and the Future Teachers of America (girls do that—no one really wants to be a teacher), and I listen to all kinds of music and I even play the piano a little and I'm on the tennis team. (That's a *lot* less exciting than it sounds. We only got the team last year and anyone who could identify a racket could be on it.) I don't have a boyfriend but I've been on plenty of dates. My best friends are Mary Gail Crider and Sunny (real name Sunshine, hippie parents) Hughes. Mary Gail is the skinny, bubbly one, always laughing, big teeth, potential valedictorian. Sunny is the long blond curls, vacant smile, violet eyes, future artist of some kind. I'm the one in the middle. The sturdy girl. The one who's going to do something really smart and practical like open a business, even though I secretly dream of being in a rock band or being a poet in San Francisco. I don't know why I think of California all the time. It just seems like a place I could live. I don't know why I've never been comfortable here in the South, even though I've never known anything else. It just seems like some place has to be better. Maybe that's just my circumstances. I'd like to get your impression, but that is not going to happen. We aren't going to meet and chat like normal people. I'm never going to do anything like a normal person except impersonate one for a little bit longer.

Back to the criminal thing, I'll bet you're saying. That is if you're still reading, if you haven't decided it's all a big tasteless joke and thrown the whole mess into the fire.

I'd like to say it all started last summer or the summer before or anything neat and tidy like that, a perfect date I could mark off on my calendar every year, like an anniversary. It's nothing like that. It all started a long time before me. That's what I realize now. All criminals are a long time in the making. They don't just spring up. They gestate like babies. No, more complicated and more deliberate. They are carved out of history, like a custom-made table out of a big piece of oak. Care and precision. The right place at the right time, and everything working in its favor, like the elements of a storm coming together.

It didn't start with me and it didn't even start with my parents. It might not even have started with my grandparents. That's why I have to give you a short history of Union Grade.

You could probably use that, since the rumor is you're from up North. New York, some say. D.C. according to others. I can't tell from looking at you, though the long hair and the cool hats and the ripped jeans and the leather bracelets and the general aloof swagger make me vote for New York. You're really handsome but not stuck-up, probably because, where you come from, a lot of guys looked like you and it was no big deal. Down here at Union Grade High, you are stirring things up if you haven't noticed. Which you don't seem to. Girls bruise each other's ribs when you walk past, and you must notice that sudden flurry of whispers that trail you like a lapdog. You must but you don't appear to. You just walk along, looking for your class numbers and speaking when spoken to. Jimmy English, who's been my friend since the sandbox, says he has phys ed with you and that you're the only guy there who can do twenty pull-ups, and that you ran the second-fastest mile, after Kirby Dwight, who's a track star. You wouldn't know it to look at him, Jimmy said, but the dude is fast. So you've already earned the respect of your male peers, if you care to take advantage of it. And the drop-dead-at-your-feet admiration of any girl you want. Please don't get too aware of that.

Oh, what do I care? Do what you want. Just try to

choose someone good. Like Mary Gail. She's so nice if you can get her to stop talking. Sunny's a bit too artsy vague. She'd drive you crazy.

And I, of course, am going to jail.

So back to the history of this place you've moved to.

As you can see, we're right on the North Carolina line, but that doesn't mean we're anything like the Carolinians—far from it. We're wickedly territorial on both sides, deeply offended if we're mistaken for the other. It's a history of grudges and resentment and one state thinking it's classier than the other. We're both hicks, let's face it, and even though I'm not given to taking sides, you have to admit Virginia is the Home of the Presidents. We have George Washington and Thomas Jefferson and James Madison and all those people who started the whole country, so I think we do win in the classier category. Not that the founding fathers had anything to do with Union Grade. They were in Williamsburg and northern Virginia, mostly. Union Grade was not even a spot on the map until well after the Revolution. It existed but it was nothing more than a store and a church and a village. It didn't have a name. It finally got a charter in 1780 and it was called Competition, because that's what it hoped to be—real competition for the next town over, a place called Schoolfield, because it had a school and is now called Danville, after the river it sits on, the Dan River.

Then came the Civil War. We lost. That's all you need to know about that.

Then came Reconstruction. Competition, like any small Southern town, was at the complete mercy of the

North. When the Union soldiers, the Reconstruction workers, the "carpetbaggers," as they were known around here, came down to divide up the goods, they had a system of grading what they found—everything from land to horses to houses to women. Top-notch stuff was marked "Union Grade." There was so much good stuff in Competition that it basically became known as a Union Grade town, and then, after the horrors of Reconstruction were ended by President Rutherford B. Hayes, it started regaining its independence but kept the name.

Hold on, freak, you're thinking. What's a sophomore doing with all that information? Listening in class? Not likely. My teacher, Mr. Roberts, is so boring we can hardly keep our eyes open, except to stare when he's writing on the board because he does have a nice butt. (He's the football coach. I won't continue with this train of thought.) The thing is, my father is a history buff. He reads it all the time. He retains it. Then he talks to me about it when I'm helping him in the garden, or when he's pointing out birds to me, or when we're playing golf. He has a lot of interests and he shares them with me. That's because I'm his favorite. "My idea," he tells me. Which means my mother didn't want to have me. He doesn't get why that might be a sensitive subject to me. I've never let on that it's painful.

My father shares all these things with me because I was supposed to be a boy. The fact that I wasn't didn't stop him from raising me as one. Sometimes it's confusing, even hurtful, but I'm grateful for the stuff I've learned. I can identify just about any variety of plant, I can build a birdhouse, I can drive the green with a four iron on a three par with a good tailwind. I can tell you about different kinds of wood or how to start a fire or how to stop one or how a printing press works or how to get paint off the floor. I can name a lot of presidents and I know what the Marshall Plan was. It goes on and on like this. I usually keep it to myself. You're the unwilling recipient of everything I've learned from him.

What's funny (funny strange, not funny haha) is that by casually telling me about history—of this place, of the country, of our family—he was inadvertently responsible for helping me understand what I needed to know to put the whole puzzle together. Even though he never dreamed I'd put it together.

He still doesn't know.

I realize I'm not going to finish this in one sitting. I have created this space behind a board in my closet for when I have to put it aside. I know I am going to worry about it whenever I am away. But there's no other choice. That's the thing about a dead end. When you get to it you can only look two ways—back where you've come from, or up. Up is the sky, the only way to go, but you can't entirely see how to get there. Then you find the ladder.

I have to stop now. My mother is calling me to dinner.

I put the letter aside and leaned back on my bed and felt exhausted. U2 was singing about something to do with God and I took the iPod off because I couldn't stand it, couldn't absorb anything else smart or sensitive.

I took deep breaths into my stomach the way the yoga

teacher at school told us to do. We all made fun of her, but I had to admit, it made my heart stop racing and I felt these weird chemicals going off in my brain. I needed to calm down and put things in perspective. I had to keep telling myself that this was my mother talking. It didn't sound like her. But she sounded like someone I would have wanted to hang out with. She was smarter than me. She knew things about history and she could put them in order and relate them to herself. When I was taught California history in the fifth grade, the only thing that seemed to affect my life was the founding of In-N-Out Burger. I couldn't draw a line from the Spanish missions or Lewis and Clark or Woody Guthrie to my existence in the Pacific Palisades.

But my mother had an understanding of how the Civil War affected her. She was on the wrong side of it, obviously. And in American History, we didn't waste much time on the losers. No one cared what happened to the people who fought and died to protect slavery. So I had never really learned much about Reconstruction in the South. I tried to imagine her ancestors having their homes and families raided by opportunists from the North, being marked up and graded and divided. Regardless of their political positions, these were actual people, families with children, and whether I liked it or not, these were my relatives. I shared their DNA.

I liked this girl (my own mother, actually) who knew and cared about her history. It made me want to know and care about mine. But I was afraid to look.

I was hoping when I finally got to the point, her crime would be something really slight, not horrible at all, something that had just grown horrible in her imagination, like the time I was in second grade and was convinced I was going to jail for losing a library book. It took me ages to confess it. My mother found me sobbing in my room one morning and finally coaxed the transgression out of me, and when I blurted it out she started laughing. I remember her hugging me and all that guilt and weight just melted and I felt she had magical powers.

That person could not have done anything really bad.

I thought for a moment about skipping ahead, but I knew I couldn't. I had to read it exactly the way this Noah guy had read it. He probably didn't have to put it down periodically, because it wasn't his mother—just some stranger to him.

I put the letter back under the bed and went for my cell phone to call Jen. Then I looked outside and saw that it had gotten gray and windy. The surf was too big and I didn't actually want to hurt myself.

Another activity came to mind. There was only one place that could make me feel as calm and as connected and as churned up and alive as the ocean.

· 3 ·

I never told anyone how much I enjoyed the cemetery. No one even knew I went there. Except Jen, and I let her believe it was a rare event. But it was a routine.

I would take the bus into Westwood at least once a week. I would stop and get flowers and a Snapple and some Twizzlers. (My mom loved Twizzlers.) Then I would walk to the cemetery and sit near her grave and start talking to her as if she were actually present. Nobody paid attention. No one was around in the middle of the day. And I felt everything inside of me calming down. She was very real for me there. I was convinced she could hear me.

I knew it didn't make any sense. If she was in heaven, if such a place existed, then she could hear me wherever I was. The ground and the grave and the ornate marker didn't make her more available. But it worked for me. I let myself be irrational about it.

My father would bring me here on the anniversary of her death, but we didn't talk to her. We just stood and stared at the ground and at the flowers and the sky. Then we left. I wondered if he made his own secret visits. But I didn't ask him. I was too busy trying to take care of his emotions. I was afraid to see him cry.

Enough time had passed now that I felt really young when my mother died. For years it seemed like yesterday, then last week, then last month. Now it felt like a different time. When I was little. I didn't feel little anymore.

In the early days, I'd pray for her to come back, and that was painful. Because I was just old enough to know she couldn't, but young enough to believe in all kinds of magic, like Santa Claus and God.

Then I dropped Santa Claus and got mad at God.

Then I stopped believing in God.

Then I got mad at my father.

Then the guy who hit my mother, the bad drunk driver who was in jail.

Then I stopped being mad at everybody and felt very sorry for myself.

Then I dropped all that and just had a quiet sadness deep down, like the one I remembered my mother having.

Now I could stand there at her grave and not blame anybody. I could just know that life happened that way and some people got unlucky and I was one of them. And she was one of them.

I said to the grave, "Hey, Mom, thanks for the letter. It's really tripping me out."

I pictured her smiling.

I wondered what she would look like if she had lived this long. I remembered her with perfect skin, flipped-under brown hair and laughing green eyes, freckles on her nose, hands on her hips. She never wore sweats, like the other mothers. She always put on real clothes, even if they were jeans. She used to say, "Lynnie, the end of civilization is when people stop wearing clothes with buttons and zippers." Then she'd laugh. She understood what that meant. I was just embarrassed because the other mothers wore workout clothes everywhere.

Now I realized she had been trying harder. If she had lived, she would have been one of those cool Hillsboro mothers who dressed well and did just enough work around the school but didn't wear out her welcome or become a nuisance.

"You're just trying to keep your mother perfect," Jen had said to me. She said it as if it were a character flaw, and maybe it was.

"So look," I said, "I'm reading it because Daddy said I should and I trust him. I feel like I'm eavesdropping, since I don't know this guy Noah, and I haven't gotten to the part where you explain . . ." I paused and lowered my voice to a whisper, "why you're a criminal. I guess I'm hoping that part is not really true. And I'm here to tell you that whatever you say, I'm not going to change my mind about you. Okay, maybe I'll change my mind, but I'm not going to stop, you know, loving you."

I paused and wondered if that were true. I had never stopped loving anyone. I wasn't sure it was possible. I had stopped having crushes on people before, but that was different. Love felt like a thing you couldn't change.

"It's already weird," I said, "reading your thoughts when you were my age. Well, just a little bit younger. You weren't old enough to drive a car yet. I am old enough but as it turns out, I don't have one. I'm sure you'd disagree with Dad on this point. You guys would have one of your whispery fights that you always tried to hide from me. I didn't mind them. I could tell they weren't very serious."

I took a breath and glanced up at the trees, which were bowing and dancing under the low gray skies, so untypical of L.A. this time of year. But it always felt more fitting to be in the graveyard when the weather was gloomy. I was about to start my next speech when I noticed someone nearby, staring at me. At first glance he seemed like a nerdy tourist. He was sitting next to a tombstone with a sketchbook in his lap. He had boxes of charcoal pencils surrounding him, but he wasn't drawing. He was just staring at me. I stared back at him.

He lifted a hand to me in a casual wave, and I remembered him from yesterday. He was sitting in that exact spot, doing that exact thing when Jen and I came by.

I stared at him unapologetically, trying to decide if he was a graveyard freak, a stalker, or just someone with a dead relative, like me.

He was about my age, though it was hard to tell by the way he was dressed. He wore jeans and the same fatigue jacket (thrift shop, it seemed to me, instead of Abercrombie, intentionally distressed) and some ratty denim shirt and Converse sneakers beaten up and written on. His hair was dark blond, somewhere between too long and not long enough, and from this distance it looked as if he actually had a reason to shave. His eyes were a scary, unfinished blue and they were staring right at me.

I walked toward him, close enough to be heard.

"Am I bothering you?" I asked.

"Not yet," he said.

"When will you know?"

He shrugged. "When you bother me."

I turned away from him, as if I thought I could ignore him. But when I tried to talk to my mother again, I realized that all I could see was his face. I turned back around and he was drawing in the sketchbook.

"I saw you yesterday," I said.

"Yeah. I saw you, too. And the surfer chick."

"How'd you know she was a surfer chick?"

"You always know with them."

"I happen to surf, too," I said. One day and one good ride counted.

"Whatever clangs your bell," he said, and smiled. I had to admit, it was an amazing smile.

"What are you doing here?" I asked.

"Drawing," he said.

"In a place like this?"

He shrugged again. "Sure."

"Doesn't it occur to you that people come here to talk to their dead relatives?"

"That's okay with me."

"Why do you like to draw here?"

"It's usually quiet. I like quiet."

"Have you been listening to me?"

"Not really."

"I suppose you think it's weird, somebody talking to a grave."

"Not really. It happens a lot."

He put his sketchbook aside and looked up at me. He had kind of an angelic face and I wondered for a brief, insane moment if he might actually be an angel. Such strange ideas occurred to me when I was in the graveyard. But I figured angels didn't need to shave.

"What's your name?" I asked.

"Mick."

"Oh," I said. "As in Jagger."

"Yeah, I was named after him."

My eyebrows went up. "Your parents knew him or something?"

He laughed. "My father probably thought he did when he was high. My old man died of an overdose when I was too little to know him. I live with my mom. She doesn't talk about him much."

I didn't say anything. He got to his feet and walked in my direction. He was taller than me.

"What's your name?" he asked.

"Lynne. Where do you go to school?"

"Uni High," he said, nodding roughly in the direction of the

43

high school a few streets away. A public high school. There were rumors about it. All the kids were wild. But that was the rumor about all the kids who didn't go to private school.

"How about you?" he asked.

"Hillsboro."

"Oh, okay," he said, passing judgment.

I wanted to tell him I was a scholarship kid, just to ease the tension. But it didn't seem right to lie, standing on my mother's grave.

He said, "So your parents are what, rich showbiz types?"

"My father's a lawyer. My mother's right here," I said, pointing to the ground.

"I see. That's who you're talking to."

"Yeah."

He was close to me now. We stared at each other. A weird kind of calm came over me as I looked at his face.

"What do you have against Hillsboro girls?" I asked.

"It's what they have against me," he said. "Not the other way around."

"What were you drawing?" I asked, not knowing what else to do.

"I'll show you if you want to see."

I followed him to where he had been sitting. He picked up the sketchbook, flipped through a few pages, and showed it to me. It was a pretty good abstract drawing of a graveyard. The tombstones looked like teeth, all crooked and carnivorous. The limbs of the trees reached down like magical wires.

"I like to look at death," he said, "and take all the mystery out of it. My goal is to make a drawing of a graveyard and it doesn't look any more interesting than, I don't know, man-nequins in a store."

"You're not there yet," I said.

He turned the sketchbook toward himself and laughed.

"No, I guess not."

I laughed, too. It was the first time I could remember actu-ally laughing, standing so close to my mother.

I looked at my watch.

"I have to go," I said. "I have to catch the bus. I don't have a car."

He smiled. "That's unusual for a Hillsboro girl."

"Tell me about it."

"Okay," he said. "Maybe I'll see you here again."

"Unlikely," I said.

He shrugged. "Meeting you was unlikely. I figure we're past the hurdle."

• 4 •

By the time I got home my dinner was cold and my father was glaring.

"I was about to call the police," he said.

"No, you weren't."

"Yes, Lynnie, I was. I called Jen's parents and they said she wasn't surfing. So I knew you weren't either. Because surely you wouldn't do anything that stupid."

"Am I branded as a troubled kid now? I skipped one day of school."

"It worries me to see you acting this way."

"Hey, the big letter was your idea."

He stood very still and said, "This is about the letter?"

"Maybe."

"How much have you read?"

"Not much."

He shook his head and said, "Maybe it was a mistake."

"Too late now."

"Lynnie, I only have my own judgment. I don't have a partner to run it by."

"I went to see Mom. In the cemetery."

This gave him the slightest pause. He knew he couldn't argue, but he had to say something.

"You should have left a note."

"I was in a hurry."

"Hurry? What hurry?"

"I had to catch the bus. As in I don't have a car. Remember?"

"My God, is this about the car?"

"No, actually, it's about the letter. Did you think it was going to be easy for me?"

"No," he said.

A minute passed of us staring at each other. He ran his fingers through his hair and sighed. "Maybe it's for when you're older. I should take it back."

"You can't."

"You're right," he said. "It's done."

"I'm going to bed," I told him.

"You have to eat."

"No, I don't."

"Let's not throw anorexia into the mix, all right?"

"Stop reading magazines. You can lose your appetite without having an eating disorder."

"Lynnie . . ."

"Dad. Stop. It's okay."

He looked at me and I smiled at him and I saw his shoulders relax. I felt for him. I wouldn't want to be raising me alone.

I got ready for bed and got the letter out again.

Before I started reading I paused to think of Mick standing in the graveyard, smiling at me. I wondered if he was really cute or I was just desperate. We weren't around boys much at Hillsboro. Sometimes they threw us together with the Loyola boys at a lame dance, where we all stood on opposite sides of the room. Two or three couples would venture to dance right before it was all over. The more sophisticated girls would actually get phone numbers or e-mails. The rest of us sat near the refreshments and gossiped or mocked.

The point is, I was boy-experience impaired. And I might have been giving Mick some qualities he didn't possess. But then I remembered his smile and I knew I wasn't entirely making it up.

The memory of him made me feel strong. So I took a yoga breath and read.

September 27
Dear Noah,

English class was boring today. We had a quiz and spent the rest of the class reading silently. I admit that I stole looks at you but you never noticed. It's just as well.

Sometimes when I look at you, I imagine us getting acquainted and even going on dates. I'd love it, but it's not going to happen. And that's why I keep writing. My whole life I've been watching the happy children, accepting that I can't be one of them.

And, then, knowing what I know about you.

So back to where I left off. Well, I left off in several places. I left off at the history of me and my father, as well as the history of Union Grade right after Reconstruction. I suppose history of the place should come first.

Imagine the shape this town was in right after Reconstruction. That brings us up to the late eighteen hundreds. The South was defeated, in spirit and economy, but Reconstruction was over and Union Grade was trying to establish itself again. The industries were trying to find foot, the slaves were freed and trying to figure out how to live, the battle-worn families were trying to reclaim their dignity, defeated and terrified and suddenly poor.

Now let's travel a bit down the road to Hadley Creek, an area that fared a bit better in Reconstruction. Somehow, the farmers held on to their land—rumor had it they made deals with the devil or worse, with the carpetbaggers.

Let's start with Mom's side. The rich side.

The Brodies of Hadley Creek.

Meet my mother's father, my maternal grandfather, Grandpa Will Brodie, of remote Scottish descent. He was born to a wealthy landowner, a gentleman farmer, John Brodie. Will was the youngest of several sons and was impatient to have his portion of the land handed down. He somehow earned the money and bought his share of the farm as well as a brother's share.

This was a deal with the devil, by all accounts. The money probably came from bootlegging, and he took advantage of his family's debts during a period of drought. So he got the money but was disowned by the family. All shrouded in a mystery we don't need to solve right now. That brings us up to the turn of the century. Grandpa Brodie was in possession of a small farm and was looking to have his own family. He was inventive, wealthy, and a bit of a rapscallion.

Now the rumors really run wild. Some say he married a distant relative, the beautiful olive-skinned Nancy Jukes, heir to a distant North Carolina fortune. Other stories say that he met Nancy in a bar in North Carolina, where she was earning a living as a lounge singer. Nobody really knows anything except that my grandmother, Granny Nancy, was exotically lovely, darker than any self-respecting white girl should be. A no-nonsense girl who was happy to marry "up," which is Southern for improving her circumstances. She took easily to being a wealthy farmer's wife.

They quickly had three children—my mother, Fern, first. She was black-haired and black-eyed, gorgeous and petulant and wild. My aunt Rose second—blond and fair-skinned and fair-natured, no trouble at all. And then my uncle Joseph, dark like my mother and nothing else to recommend him except that he was a boy.

Grandpa Will didn't care for the girls. He only wanted a boy, and as soon as he got one he forgot all about the sisters. Mama Nancy did her best with the wild girl and the shy one, but as soon as they were free to marry she let them. Fern got married first, before she even left high school, to the handsomest boy in town, named Gerard Wyatt.

Fern became my mother. So that's what we'll call her from this point on.

Mama always said she married right away to get out of her house. I don't know what that means; I don't ask her. She was happy in her marriage at first. Gerard made a lot of money as a tobacco salesman, and it wasn't long before they had a son, my much older brother, Gregory. Their style of high living calmed right down after that. Whereas they used to run around the Southeast, taking vacations and going to parties, Mama was forced to stay at home with Gregory. Her husband kept running around.

Not long after one of his "business" trips, Mama received a pair of shoes in the mail. A note accompanying the shoes said, "Mrs. Wyatt, you left these in the hotel room during your last stay."

"They weren't even my size," Mama told me when she related the story. My sister and I used to laugh very hard at the tale and Mama laughed too, just to keep us company. But I could see she didn't find it funny.

Mama moved out of her married home and back in with her parents. Only, they didn't want her. My grandfather had spent his whole life trying to get the girls out of the house—damned if he was going to take the difficult one back in. My grandmother always sided with him. She said, "No way, Miss Sister, you made your bed, you've got to lie in it."

It was 1952. Mama was all alone in the world with a little boy, barely four years old. She didn't know how to cope. Grandma suggested that she move to Danville to find a job. They would look after Gregory until she situated herself. When she found herself a job and a husband, she could have her son back. My mother agreed. There was nothing else she could do.

"Looking back, I should have seen how it was going to go," Mama used to say to me. "But I didn't know what else to do. I didn't have anybody to teach me."

She got all dreamy when she said things like that, as if she had somehow missed her own life.

She doesn't talk about it much anymore. This was when I was little. These days she just sits and smokes and drinks iced tea and writes letters to Sandra in college. When she sees me it's like she's a little confused as to why I'm still around.

Don't go feeling sorry for me—that's not the point and I've done nothing to deserve it. I'm just telling you how it is in my family.

When my mother went off to Danville to look for that job, she was still young and beautiful and all full of hope. She had made a mistake but she hadn't ruined her life. Ruining your life takes time and work and one wrong decision after another. She hadn't done it yet, but she was on her way.

That's where we leave our heroine, my mother, in a boardinghouse in Danville, working as a receptionist at a newspaper, and maybe for the first time in her life feeling strong, with a sense of purpose. But missing her son. Always missing him.

Now back to Union Grade. My father's side.

The Pittmans of Union Grade.

My father's family is from the town of Competition/Union Grade as far back as anyone can remember. They actually lived in town, which meant there weren't any wealthy landowners in sight. They were workers. They worked for wages, the men and the women alike. When there was no work, they were hungry. After the war, during Reconstruction, their situation was "no better than the Negroes," my Grandma Lucille used to say. She was my father's mother, the crazy one. The genuinely crazy one; we had to visit her in the psych ward when I was little. A guy with keys would come to let us in. She would sit in her room and wring her hands. But I'm getting ahead of myself.

They were no better off than the freed slaves, these workers, my father's family, and that was a reality they just couldn't get their heads around. Before the war they at least had someone to look down on. I'm telling you this because that's how it was explained to me, not because any of it is justifiable. It's just how my father was raised. On the lowest rung of the social order. Maybe you've heard of white trash as a joke, but back then it was a real thing. On the social scale, they were below the freed slaves. Which is why they were allowed to starve.

My grandfather, Russell Pittman, who was a decent, nondrinking man, struggled to keep the family's head above water. All his brothers were drunks. Some of them had gone to jail. But he was going to keep his family respectable if it killed him.

He worked in various handyman jobs and eventually found his way to fairly steady work at a sawmill. His wife helped out by sewing for people. When the children were born, my father Clyde first, his sister Margaret second, my grandfather said no to Grandma Lucille working anymore. It was a pride issue, though they were nearly broke. A decent man in those days did not let the mother of his children work.

They got by. They were poor. The Depression came and some days they didn't eat. Neighbors helped them out. My father's memory of this time was so bleak he could hardly talk about it. He would never let us put popcorn on the Christmas tree because he said that was something born out of the Depression and it made him too sad. For the same reason we could never eat beans in my house—that was all they had sometimes growing up. He had a list of things like that. My mother was impatient about it. She couldn't understand the trauma of poverty because she had never had to confront it. "My people always had money," she would whisper to me.

My father's memory of his life growing up was spotty and irregular. Sometimes he recalled pure happiness, simple things that made him giddy and sentimental. His parents were loving and pure, easy to understand. Hard work was rewarded and they all believed in God. He played sports and looked out for his sister, and in the evenings they sat around and told stories rather than watching television (which they didn't have, obviously). Everything was elemental and no one pondered his purpose on earth. They just lived, from day to day, and it all worked. Sometimes he did recall and would remind me that it was nothing more than their "good reputation" that kept them from starving. His father taught him how to build things and how to garden, while his mother taught his sister Margaret how to cook and clean. They knew how to take care of themselves and each other.

It was a nice, idealized vision, but it didn't strike anyone he told as particularly true. My father was too tense, too worried, too tortured to have come from the family that he described. And he knew, as we all did, that my grandmother's hold on sanity was not entirely secure. It never had been. She had been in and out of reality for as long as anyone could recall.

When my father was a mere eight years old, he had been out in the yard playing baseball when he started to get a little bit tired and achy. His mother called him in, sent him to bed, and then called the doctor. The doctor came (the only doctor in town who made house calls back then) and examined him and decided that he had rheumatic fever, one of those strange diseases of the heart common in those days. For an entire year after that, my father stayed in bed. Not in his room, mind you, in bed. An entire year. He read comic books and learned how to draw, but he did not leave his bed. As a result, he missed a lot of things, like learning how to swim or ride a bike. From that moment on, his mother watched him like a hawk. He was barely allowed to play with the other boys in town. When he was a teenager, he would attempt to go to the movies with his friends, but if it happened to thunder, his mother would suddenly appear at the theater and drag him back home.

"She was crazy," my mother told me. "And she was determined to make him crazy, too."

I tried to imagine it. The best, most permanent image I had of Grandma Lucille was of her sitting in her room in the locked quarters of the psych ward, wringing her hands and crying. I tried to imagine my father, my strong, tall father, trying to become a man under her watch. It was almost impossible to picture.

"Your grandpa was a good man," Mama said, speaking of Grandpa Pittman, "but he wasn't strong enough to override her. His first wife died on their honeymoon. He never got over her. He only married your grandmother because he didn't know what else to do. He settled. But he was completely shut down, his whole life."

You had to take my mother's assessment of the whole thing with a grain of salt. She never liked my grandma Lucille, and Lucille never entirely liked or trusted her. It wasn't the woman she imagined her son marrying. If she had even been sane enough to imagine such a thing.

But before we get to that. Aunt Margaret did well in school and went to college and eventually met and married a man from Georgia and moved there. Before all that happened, though, a curious and life-altering thing happened to my father.

He had graduated from high school and was working at a gas station in town. He had grown tall and very handsome and he spent all the money he made on nice clothes. The girls loved him. He was living it up. He could see an entire future for himself, and why not? His life was turning easy, because of his job and his looks and his clothes. He hadn't really established himself in Union Grade because that was a long, hard climb. He was from hunger and this was a town full of old money types, landowners and pre–Civil War gentility who still half expected to regain the respect of the rest of the world. They mainly aspired to this by closing ranks and refusing to let the likes of my father in. But he had a plan. He would work hard enough, dress well enough, be handsome enough, and perhaps marry well enough to rise up through the social heirarchy. He was just a poor boy in a rich place, but he could see a way in through his own talents, a tiny crack of light under the door, and he was heading for it. If nothing else, he was blessed by his own countenance, his own beauty. He was one of the pretty people—a random throw of the genetic dice, but one, he had learned, that wielded a certain amount of power.

Who knows what would have happened to my father if he had simply been allowed to pursue that course. Women loved him. Even the rich women. He courted them. He was a man about town. He had charm. Doors opened for him. But he was still poor and it was still going to be a struggle. He was prepared for it. He was ready to do battle. I can only imagine how he felt in those days. The same people who frowned on him and kept him out and saw him as a poor laborer were suddenly forced to confront him. He wanted in and he was not going to take no for an answer. I admire his spirit in that regard. I'm not sure if I would have had the kind of resolve that he did in those days.

Then he was drafted. It was 1951 and the Korean War was going full force. The notice came in the mail. He told me more than once, "It was like a nightmare when I opened that letter." He was sitting in the kitchen, as he told it, and his mother said something like, "Tell them you're too sick to go," but he knew he wasn't sick, knew he hadn't actually had rheumatic fever, but was simply the victim of a nervous and crazy mother, and a lazy doctor. Maybe something about that made him want to go.

He went off to Colorado to boot camp. I'm not entirely sure what happened there. He trained for battle, that's for sure. He told me enough about that. But then there was a test. Some kind of aptitude test. They found out a few things about my father. One was that he had an above-average IQ. The other was that he was particularly gifted in the area of language and radio skills. They sent him off to Alaska to be in a special part of the army.

This part he couldn't tell me much about. "I'm not supposed to talk about it, even now," he said to me sometimes. But Alaska was the best part of his life, he often said, and it was because he had been identified as special and smart and a cut above the rest of the guys who were being shipped off to Korea and were "dropping like flies."

A couple of years ago, when I was helping him clean my Barbies and other toys out of the garage, he came across his army jacket from his Alaska days. It looked like a plain old army jacket, but with fur on the collar and a big embroidered image of a grizzly bear on the back. He glanced around as if we were possibly being observed and said, "I did special things in the war."

"Oh, yeah?" I asked.

He nodded and put a finger to his lips. He went to another box and pulled a machine out and put it down in front of me. It looked like a kind of adding machine, except there were strange, unrecognizable keys on it. He said, "Do you know what this is?"

"No," I said.

"It's a code machine."

"What kind of code?"

He said, "That's what I did in the war. I was a code-breaker."

"Oh," I said.

"Don't tell anyone that I told you. I'm not supposed to talk about it."

"Okay," I said.

I didn't have any desire to talk about it. By then I already knew things about him. Many things I wasn't supposed to talk about. But the code machine gave me a clue as to how it all happened. How I ended up where I am now, writing this letter to you.

He said, "They wanted me to stay in the army. They promised me a future. But I didn't want it. I just wanted to come back home and have a normal life."

"Come back home to be with his mama," my mother would say, on the odd occasions when his lost career in the military was being discussed. "He could be a colonel or a general by now. But he couldn't leave his mama."

"It's true what your mother says," he told me, that night we were cleaning out the garage. "I should have pursued my career, but I was afraid. Afraid that my mother needed me. I should have been braver than that."

I didn't know how to get in the middle of it. I didn't know how to intervene. It all seemed a long, long way from me. I had no idea it was the whole reason why my life had turned upside down.

After two years being a codebreaker in Alaska, my father was honorably discharged from the army and he came back home. He knocked on the door of his childhood home in the middle of the night. He told me how shocked he was when his parents came to the door. They were old, he said. He left them looking one way, and he came back to find them looking another, with gray hair and sagging faces. They hugged him and fixed him something to eat, but the whole night he was in shock. Shocked to be out of the army, shocked to have old parents, shocked to be back in Union Grade with no clear idea of who he was or what he was supposed to do.

For a long time after that, he didn't know how to get his life back together. When he was in the army, he was somebody. He was important. He did special, important work but he couldn't talk about it. He had been sworn to secrecy, even after he left the army. He was looked down upon, he said, because he hadn't seen combat. There were guys from his town, guys he'd played basketball with in high school, who had either died or come home with limbs missing or other debilitating injuries. They glared at him as if he'd done nothing special, as if he'd gotten a free pass. He couldn't even tell them; he couldn't tell anyone what he'd done. He was prohibited from explaining that his work was the most special work of all. He'd gone to Alaska because he was smarter and better. But upon his return, he was treated as if he'd simply found the coward's way out.

He didn't know what to do. For a long time, he just hung around town and went riding with his friends, looking for girls. Eventually he got a job in the local bank as a teller. He put his time in during the day, but in the evenings he went partying with his friends. There were girls, a lot of them. He was allowed to wear his uniform for a few months after service, but eventually he had to hang it up and then he really was no one at all.

The frustration festered inside of him. He had gone places and seen things. He had been in Alaska, where he learned to cross-country ski, where he learned to drive a jeep on ice, where he learned all the rules of defending against frostbite. Because he was in Intelligence, he learned other things, too, aside from radio skills. He learned how to build bombs and how to defuse them. He learned to start fires and put them out. He learned how to kill a man with his bare hands. He learned how to survive in the wilderness. He learned how to shoot a gun in the dark with gloves on. The list went on. He knew things that he would never be able to use in Union Grade. Still they treated him like a poor laborer, when he knew in his heart he was a specially skilled soldier.

Time passed and he began to think about getting married. He was getting nowhere in Union Grade. Being a bank teller brought in a steady wage, and it helped him support his parents, with whom he was still living, but it did nothing to carve out his special niche, the one he felt he had earned during his time in the army. He was still being treated like a rube, like a no one, because he couldn't speak of his special skills. It drove him to distraction. Maybe marrying the right woman would earn him his rightful place. Maybe that was what he needed.

Perhaps all these things had been in his mind the night he met my mother in a bowling alley in Danville. He was out with friends. They met up with some other people. My mother was among them. She had a job as a receptionist for the local newspaper then. She was probably feeling secure and powerful. When I was a little girl I asked my father why he married my mother. He said, "Because I thought she was the most beautiful woman I'd ever seen. And I still think so."

Even as a little girl, I knew that wasn't a good reason to marry someone.

But it was his reason.

Of their meeting, my mother only said, "I thought he was stuck-up."

Apparently, they circled around each other for a while, and then he finally asked her out and they went out and the romance started.

In my mind, he had on his uniform when he first saw her. I like it that way. She saw this handsome soldier. It can't be true—at least a year had passed since he had gotten out of the service. But I remember what my mother always said: "He was just out of the army and he was so handsome."

So these two beautiful people found each other in their beautiful clothes and something inside both of them clicked. Maybe they each saw their imagined future. I know my mother saw the man who could take care of her and help her get her son back. My father probably saw a difficult and lovely woman who would never bore him. Maybe he even saw, at last, the woman who would help him break away from his mother. Whatever forces aligned on that night, these two people saw a potential way out, and they lunged at it.

And they became my parents.

Good stopping point. I was exhausted.

I put the letter aside and turned off the light.

I lay in the dark for a long time thinking about it, this sudden and profound history lesson. My parents never talked about their past; it was as if they didn't have one. I used to ask my mother about her family and she would say, "Oh, sweetie, you're never going to have to worry about them."

I didn't understand why family was something you'd have to be worried about. But I was smart enough to sense that a sad story had to be behind it all. And I didn't want to make her sad. I never liked to think of either of my parents as having strong emotions apart from joy and humor. When you're a kid, your own emotions are all you can handle. Later you let your friends have some, but that was where it ended.

The story was interesting and I had grown to like having my mother's voice so close to me. Now I felt she was under the bed, at least, instead of always under a white stone in Westwood.

I still wasn't entirely sure how any of it related to me having a car.

All I knew was that I was slowly losing my concern and the sense that I had been deprived. Maybe that was the point.

My father was not a stupid man at all.

SIXTEEN
and Two Days

• 1 •

Zoe thought it was completely Gothic that I met a boy in a cemetery.

"Things like that never happen to me," she complained.

"That's because you don't have a dead mother," Talia reminded her.

"Oh, yeah," she said, and for a moment she actually pouted and seemed jealous.

"So your dad is not kidding about the car," Zoe said. We were eating our lunches on the manicured lawn of Hillsboro. The sun was shining and I had a sudden image of what we would look like to someone like Clyde Pittman. To him I would have been one of the in crowd, one of those fancy types in Union Grade who wouldn't give him the time of day. It also made me think of Mick, and whether or not he saw me that way. I had never really thought about social classes before, never thought of myself as rich or privileged. But now it was starting to come into focus.

"No," I said. "He's not kidding. There will be no car for Little Lynnie Russo."

"That is so bizarre," Talia said. "It's tragic, really."

"It's not," I said. "I mean it sucks, but it's not tragic."

To Talia everything was tragic. And I realized that before I'd started reading the letter, I would have agreed with her.

"I see you're still rocking the bird bracelet?" Zoe asked.

I had almost forgotten it. I had slept in it and woken up with tiny little bird marks on my wrist.

"I'm starting to like it," I said. "Is that scary?"

"Pretty scary," Zoe admitted. "I mean, the birds look deformed."

"Maybe it's some kind of metaphor. Even deformed birds can fly," Talia said.

I laughed, but there was something to it.

"So rumor is you went surfing with Jen," Zoe said, "the day you ditched. Are you a surfer now? Should we prepare for the red beads and the Uggs and the lingo?"

"It was really fun. I think I'm good at it."

"Lynne, we cannot lose you to surfing," Talia insisted.

"Yeah, we'd rather lose you to the guy in the cemetery."

"You're not going to lose me to anything."

But I wasn't entirely sure about that. I was changing and I could feel it.

I stayed late at school to finish my homework. But also, I realized, because I was avoiding the letter. I wasn't afraid of it anymore. I just wanted to make it last.

My cell phone rang as I was riding home on the late bus. The number that came up was unfamiliar to me. I answered it anyway.

"Hi," he said, "it's me, the guy from the cemetery."

I laughed. "I meet a lot of guys in the cemetery."

"Mick," he said.

"I'm kidding. I don't meet guys in cemeteries."

"Oh, okay. I'm nervous."

I smiled. I thought it was cute that he admitted to being nervous.

"How did you get my number?"

He said, "I know a guy who dates a girl at Hillsboro. He got me a school roster. Your number is on there. Is that creepy? Am I stalking you?"

"Not yet. But there's time."

He laughed.

He said, "Well, I was just wondering if you wanted to get together sometime and hang out."

"In the cemetery?"

"Sure, if you want to."

"You're totally missing all my jokes."

He said, "Well, I take all my dates to the cemetery, so I thought it would make sense."

"Funny."

"So I guess I just admitted that I'm asking you on a date."

"You don't do this a lot, do you?"

"Almost never," he admitted. "I mean, I have dated. Not in cemeteries. You know, this went much better when I practiced it in my room."

"Oh, really? What did I say when you practiced it?"

"You said you'd love to go out with me sometime."

"I'd love to go out with you sometime."

"Oh, shit," he said. "I didn't practice anything after that."

"Well, let's see. Here's where you tell me what night you were thinking of and what we might do."

"I haven't thought about that, either."

"Do you want to call me back after you've rehearsed it?"

"No, no, I can think on my feet. We could see a movie. No, wait, we could get dinner. No, probably just meeting at Jamba Juice or something in Larchmont after you get out of school. And if we like each other over smoothies, then we could do something more serious."

"Like to go the cemetery."

"Right."

"Okay, when?"

"Tomorrow. Which is a Friday. That's a good day for a date."

"It's a date. See, that wasn't so hard."

He laughed. "You've done this before, haven't you?"

"No," I answered honestly. "This will be my first juice date."

"I'll see you tomorrow, Lynne," he said. A kind of electric current went through me when he said my name. I hung up the phone and settled back in the seat and smiled out the window at all the things passing. The world looked good to me.

• 2 •

When I got home, the letter was waiting, and except for a snack and a quick glance at MTV, I didn't avoid it.

September 28

Dear Noah,

You tried to talk to me as we were leaving English class today. You asked if you could look at my notes for the test next week. I told you that my notes were a mess and that you should ask someone else. You looked kind of upset. I realized that you didn't really care about the notes—you were just trying to talk to me and I blew you off. You were aware that I was blowing you off. I felt bad about it and I wanted to explain. What I would have said to you is that we can't get to know each other. The whole idea is that we don't know each other—that's why I can write the letter to you. If I get to know you, I'll have something to protect. After all, I have plenty of friends and relatives and even my pastor whom I could tell this story to. I've had the opportunity but I let it pass because by virtue of knowing me, they will want to disbelieve me. They will want it not to be true. They might even try to tell me it's not true and that would make me completely crazy, crazier than I already fear that I am.

But I'm not crazy. I'm just someone who was born into insanity. I'm sane, and this letter is my last best hope of hanging on to that.

By the way, what I want you to know when you read this is that I'm probably completely in love with you. I don't really know you so it's not entirely accurate to say that. But I love who I think you are, the person I've made up in my mind. That person is warm and funny and worldly and sweet and wise. I know you're handsome; that's not a subjective thing. It's just a fact. I just want you to know I love you for bigger reasons than that. Believe me, I have imagined it so many times—me and you in a perfect world, or at least a world in which I'm not carrying around the secret of my criminal life. In a weird way, I have to keep you at a distance and write this letter to you so you won't make the mistake of falling in love with me, too. Because you can't have me. I can't have you. I'm damaged goods. I'm the wrong girl for reasons you can't even imagine. I am the enemy.

It would have been nice. I want you to know that. You and me holding hands at assembly or at a movie. Us being a couple. Noah and Cat, Cat and Noah. I think about it all the time. It stirs up the same feeling I always had watching kids playing on the playground, on the monkey bars and the swing set and the slide. They get to do that because they aren't me. Because they don't know what I know. They haven't done what I've done.

And I also want to tell you that never in a million years did I ever think you'd be interested in me. That was not in the game plan.

But I digress.

Now for the story of my brother.

My brother Gregory is twelve years older than I am, the product of my mother's first marriage. He's a half brother but that hardly matters. He is a minister in North Carolina and he's married to a very nice woman named Suzanne. They don't have any kids yet. We see them periodically. They come to visit and the visits are always stiff and awkward. He doesn't know my mother well, because she didn't raise him, and he resents (I suspect) me and my sister because my mother did raise us. You can imagine his position. Why were we good enough for her and he wasn't? He doesn't have any perspective on it, that's the problem. The person who does have perspective is his wife, Suzanne. She gave me a lot of the history I'm about to tell you.

I realize I'm bad at creating suspense because now I've revealed that my mother never got her son back. He was raised by my grandparents. My parents had me and my sister, but Gregory's relationship to our family remained sporadic. We saw him when we drove to the farm to see my grandparents every other Sunday. He stayed with us now and then and always at Christmas. But by the time I was seven he was married (he married very young) and in seminary. After that, he moved around a lot because that's how a preacher's life works. He was handsome and charming and charismatic (he looked a little like you, to be honest) and I adored him, but we just didn't have much of a relationship. It took some time, but eventually I understood why, mostly through Suzanne's stories. He has a lot of anger toward my mother, but that's because he doesn't know the whole story. For some reason, I'm the person in possession of the whole story. Maybe that burden always falls on the youngest. And it's a very heavy burden.

Here is what I know of the next part of my parents' lives, after they met in the bowling alley. Some of it I'm guessing at and most of it is culled from family dinners after Suzanne had had too much wine and started to talk, but only to me. Maybe she thought I was too young to remember or understand. But I've always been able to retain things.

My father began to court my mother in the usual way. After several dates, she revealed that she had been married before and had a son. He might have cared about that in the beginning, but by this point he was taken with her and he was willing to accept her history. She took him home to meet her parents and they mostly approved. They saw that he was not exactly their class (laborer versus wealthy landowners again), but he was handsome and had a decent job and, unlike a lot of men in that era, he was willing to take her on. My mother's parents were a little bit nervous because by now Gregory was seven and they had gotten used to having him and secretly had no plans to give him up. He was their son. I can imagine that my grandpa Will had sized my father, Clyde, up and decided that he was too weak to put up much of a fight. Possibly they had had some walks in the backyard and Grandpa Will had let him know that Gregory was not part of the deal. My father must have known that Fern had every intention of taking her son into the equation. But there was probably a part of my father that didn't want to take on a ready-made family. So there was a complicit agreement. Such an agreement, however, didn't make Grandfather Will entirely comfortable. He was examining his arsenal and preparing for a fight, but as it turned out, the ultimate weapon appeared out of nowhere.

About a month before my parents' wedding took place, a woman in Union Grade came forth, claiming to be pregnant by my father. It was a scandal on a plate. Getting a woman pregnant in those days was a dark deed, something that mainly occurred among the lower classes, and this only served to remind my father that he wasn't one of the elite. Suddenly he saw the whole thing slipping

71

away—he stood to lose the most beautiful woman he'd ever seen, along with the social status that her family could afford him. It's not clear if my mother ever knew about this. She was very proper and proud, and she had already left one man for cheating on her. But her parents were intent on this marriage taking place, if for no other reason than to get this wayward daughter off their hands, not to mention keeping her son in their home.

Then a backyard talk definitely took place. It went like this: My grandfather had money, and money could make anything disappear. He was willing to write a check to this troublesome young woman and make the whole issue go away. But there would be a certain price attached. One was that my father would go ahead and marry my mother and take her off their hands once and for all. The bigger price tag was that there would be no discussion of taking Gregory from them. Grandfather Will probably threw in some other perks, such as helping my father get set up in a good job, maybe even a financial contribution. But the heftiest part of the deal was that Gregory would remain with them. I can picture my father shaking on the deal, in the backyard of my grandfather's house, overlooking his prosperous farm.

The final part of the agreement was that my mother was never to know.

It was a deal with the devil. And once you make a deal with the devil, your soul is up for grabs.

I'm not entirely sure how I feel about evil, if it exists, and if it does exist, how it works. But I do think that once you sell a tiny part of your soul, you may as well sell the whole thing. You may as well have a sign over your head saying, "I can be bought."

My father was bought.

How did he feel when he walked away from that deal? I want to believe that he was just in love and hopeful and certain that he could somehow make up for it. I want to believe that some small part of his soul was still engaged and hoping for the best. He was betting on a bright future. He wasn't selling the best part of himself to the highest bidder. He had plans.

But the thing about dancing with the devil is this: You're not done dancing until the devil is done dancing. And the devil is never done.

So they got married. It was a small wedding in the Methodist church in Union Grade. My parents were dressed to the nines and they looked beautiful. My brother Gregory was a groomsman. It all looked very good and that's what they were buying into: how it looked.

The first years of their marriage are murky, uncertain years to me. Suzanne didn't provide any information as to how that went, so I can only imagine. What I imagine is this: My mother kept talking about getting Gregory back and my father kept giving her all these rational arguments as to why it was better for him to stay with his grandparents. They'd be taking him away from the life he knows. If my father adopted him, Gregory would have to change his name. They can still see him anytime they want. They're going to have their own family. As the years passed, it got harder and harder for her to get him back and she just got worn down by the arguments.

But in the back of her mind, she knew this: She only married my father to get her son back. Without that, what was he to her? He moved her away from her job in Danville and into a stifling small-town existence in Union Grade. They lived near his parents, and my father's meddling, semi-crazy mother dropped by whenever she felt like it. He wasn't making that much money, so her life was far from comfortable; she had to make sacrifices. And none of this fit in with how she saw her life evolving. She was beautiful, after all. One of the pretty people. The pretty people don't have to suffer. Yet she was suffering.

She missed her son, I imagine. She thought of him living out his life a few miles away, turning into a really spectacular young man, gifted in music and academics, with no reflection on her because she wasn't raising him. She was losing him to her parents. Deep down, her resentment grew. This was not the deal she had made. Unconsciously, she must have been aware that some other deal had been made. Some kind of secret deal that her husband would never admit to her. She lost respect for him. She wanted to go home. But she couldn't. She was trapped.

She was trapped in Union Grade, where the social class was intact. No one acknowledged her pedigree because it came from some distant place, and anyway, a woman's pedigree was only defined by her husband's achievement. They were permanently on the outside looking in. It was a place she had never been to before and she hated it. And because she hated it, she blamed my father. Nothing he could do was good enough for her. The only thing she ever really wanted him to do was get her son back.

Still, she persisted. She hung in there. A second divorce was unthinkable. She smoked, and ate very little and drank iced tea. My father insisted on having more children. She didn't want them, but he told her it was part of the deal. She agreed to get pregnant and my sister was born. She wasn't born in any typical way, though. My mother's pregnancy had been difficult. Mainly because she smoked, and ate very little and drank iced tea. My sister was born two months premature, in the car on the way to the hospital. Everything about my sister's entrance into the world was wrong. First, she was born too soon and should have died. Second, she was a girl. Third, and the most unforgivable sin, she lived.

Because it was 1957, and premature babies mostly didn't pull through back then, they just left her in the hospital and waited for her to die. They tried to get back to their lives. Every evening when he came home from work, my father would ask, "Shouldn't we go visit the baby?" And my mother would say, "I can't do that, I can't get attached, it's too painful." This went on for months, and finally my mother took a cab to the hospital, walked into the baby ward, and said, "I'm here to take my daughter home."

They had no idea who she was.

So she took my sister home and named her Sandra and started feeding her with an eyedropper. Sandra lived. But my parents never got over the fact that she lived. It wasn't their first choice. The fact that she lived forced them to confront the guilt they had about wanting her to die. My father confessed to me later that he was worried she wouldn't "look right." She looked just fine, but they could never see it. In their minds, she was always sickly and pale and flawed and just plain wrong. They also probably couldn't get over the fact that she was a girl. Imagine my mother, knowing that she had a perfectly healthy son somewhere in the world, yet here she was, stuck with raising this sickly girl. Imagine my father, knowing that he had made this deal with the devil, not being able to tell.

Imagine him blaming himself for this terrible circumstance.

Imagine my sister Sandra entering the world as a terrible circumstance, shouldering that burden.

About three years later, my father convinced my mother to have another baby. She had to; she was obligated to. This girl, Sandra, was so weak and sickly (in his mind) that he couldn't be sure she would live. So they had to have another and this one would be a boy. It must have been the boy argument that convinced my mother. She got pregnant with me and they got busy picking boy names. She carried me full term and I was born healthy and happy and squealing. But I was a girl. My father told me later that he was in shock to learn that he had had another girl. He knew it was their last because it had been so hard to convince my mother to have me. He didn't have the boy he wanted, but right then and there, in the waiting room after hearing the news, he decided that there was no reason he couldn't raise me as a boy.

They named me Catherine, but they kept my hair short as I was growing up and they dressed me in boy clothes and called me Cat because it was more boylike. That was how I ended up following my father around and hearing his stories and learning his games.

By the time I was five, my mother had come to accept that she wasn't getting her son back (he was almost grown, anyway) and her life was going to be about raising these two girls and living with a man who had completely and thoroughly lost her respect. She didn't know the whole story, but let's face it, on some level she did. But because it was too painful to really know, she shut down and smoked a lot of cigarettes and drank a lot of iced tea.

In the meantime, something had happened. My father had been lured away from his job at the bank and had been given a job in the carpet factory that was just opening up in town. A managerial position. He was offered more money and an opportunity to move up in the world. There was nothing that tempted my father more than moving up in the world. My grandfather Will probably instructed him to take the job, and he did. But it was a lousy job, where he was forced to work long hours and answer to men he didn't respect. It offered him a certain kind of social status, but it didn't fulfill his lifelong dream, which was to be completely accepted as an important member of society in Union Grade. He was allowed to join clubs and be the deacon in the church and all that, but my parents were still shut out of the best parties, the best cliques, the inner sanctum of Union Grade. By now he could see that his deal with the devil had not entirely paid off. Yet he was still in league with the devil because he had this secret. And he had an angry wife and two daughters. It was not how he saw his life playing out.

My sister and I paid the price for being daughters. My mother never really knew what to do with us. We weren't an adequate substitute for her son. And we hadn't solidified any agreement with her husband, or sealed any contract she had with her own fairy-tale vision of her life.

My sister Sandra became the focus of my mother's attention, and meanwhile, I belonged to my father. I was his last chance, his "idea," and I had certain obligations to fulfill. Because I belonged so completely to him in his mind, and because I was the closest he was ever going to get to having a son, he confided in me. He took me everywhere with him. My mother didn't mind. She was basically done with having children. She had no protective instinct toward me, so she just gave me to him. For a long time I didn't mind. I was the apple of my father's eye, his idea, his creation, his invention.

My mother was tired of it all. Tired of him, tired of missing her son, tired of raising my sister. She had no energy left for me so she let him take over. And that is why he took me with him wherever he went. And that is why I saw things I shouldn't have seen. And it's why when he decided to become a criminal, I became one, too.

All families have things they do together, like board games or silly rituals or picnics in the country. My family is no exception. From the earliest time that I can remember, whenever the town's fire alarm went off, my father woke the whole family up and said, "Let's go find it." We'd grab coats and blankets and follow him into the car. After that, we followed the trail of water that the fire truck left behind. The fire trucks in this town are really old and they leak like crazy, so that's our trail. Sometimes. And sometimes he just seemed to know how to get there.

I don't know if my mother enjoyed the adventure. I know Sandra did. It was one of the few times she actually felt like my father's daughter. She was always angling for us to act like more of a family and this did the trick for her.

My mother was just glad to get out of the house and glad that my father was in a good mood. It was unsettling how happy it made him, going to watch the fires.

For me, it was a little bit of everything. It was a completely different experience from where I was sitting.

Sometimes when we'd visit the fire, it would be a place I'd never seen before. I felt strangely happy when that was the case. My father would get out of the car and go chat with the cops or the firemen, all of whom he knew—they went to our church or belonged to the same clubs—and then he'd come back and say, "Lightning," or "Electrical system," or "Cigarette in the couch."

But many times, at least half the time, it was a place I had seen before, earlier in the day. A place he had taken me to and told me to wait in the car while he walked around it. And then it was night and the whole family was in the car and we were watching it burn. Once when I was very little, I actually said out loud, "Daddy, you took me here!" The look he gave me shut me up and made me realize I couldn't ever talk about such a thing again. The things we did together were for us to know. That's what made it a secret life.

You're probably thinking, Oh, now I get it, her father was an arsonist. That's her confession. I really wish that were the whole story. It would be terrible to have a father who was an arsonist, but it wouldn't make me feel like the criminal that I am. After all, many of the fires he started weren't important. Just old, worn-out buildings that probably needed burning down anyway. It was a way for him to demonstrate this power he had, the power he had been sitting on for all those years, the skills he had learned in the army that he could never reveal. It was a strange kind of shout to the people who wouldn't let him in.

I don't know how it made him feel better to do that. I can just barely understand it. But I know he needs it and he's going to keep doing it, just to show that he can.

There were other things, too, other parts of our secret life. I knew about the hidden family. He occasionally went to visit the woman who had his baby. She had been paid off but she had had the kid anyway, and sometimes he took me to visit them. She lived in a trailer and I would wait in the car while he went in to see her. Once she came out. She was blond and fat and looked nothing like my mother. She leaned into the window and said, "Oh, Clyde, she looks just like you." Then a girl a little older than Sandra came out and looked at me with this blank expression and told me her name was Amy. I didn't know who she was but I knew.

"This is between us," my father told me later. "We have a different connection, you and me. We're not the same as the others."

I knew he meant my mother and sister. He didn't get specific then. When I was older, he told me more.

"Your mother is crazy," he said. "Doctors have told me that I should have her put away. I think it was Sandra who did it to her. That whole experience broke her. I thought maybe having another baby . . ."

He got sentimental and sad when he talked about it. His eyes welled up. And I was young and I loved him and I wanted to make it better, but it also somehow gave me a stomachache.

"But after you she was just as crazy, and I was afraid of raising two girls by myself. So I'm just trying to make her comfortable, help her get along."

I waited for more. He wiped a tear. I didn't know what to do.

"And Sandra will never be right, I'm afraid," he said.

I didn't know what to do with any of this.

Then he turned to me with a big smile and said, "But you and me, we're the same. We're going to be okay."

We're the same, he said. He just made up his mind. I never had a choice.

I kept the secret of the fires. No one was really getting hurt. Then I let myself not think about it. Then it was exactly like it wasn't true.

But Jaqueline was different. That was a thing that never left me and never will.

I'm tired now, but tomorrow I will tell you about Jaqueline.

I put the manuscript down and sat on my bed, taking yoga breaths through my nose. It was a lot to absorb, for sure, but I had finally gotten to a point in the manuscript that made my blood stand still in my veins.

I walked down the hall to my father's room. It was dark in there. He had turned off the light and gone to sleep. But I switched it on and he sat up, looking around, all confused.

"What's happening?" he said.

"You tell me."

"Lynnie?"

"Who's Jaqueline?"

He rubbed his eyes and tried to focus on me.

"Oh," he said. "You got to that part."

"Yes, I got to that part."

He patted the bed and said, "Sit down."

"No. Just tell me."

He sighed and said, "It's in the letter. Who Jaqueline is."

"You know what I mean."

He said nothing.

"That's my name."

My real name was Jaqueline Julia Russo. Lynne was the nickname they agreed to call me. Jaqueline was so far in the past I didn't even put it down on forms anymore. But I knew it in the back of my mind.

"There was another Jaqueline before me?"

He nodded.

"Am I named after her?"

"Yes," he said, without hesitation.

"Why?"

"It's in the letter."

"Stop with the letter. Just tell me."

"Please sit down," he said.

I sat on the edge of the bed, but just barely, as if the bed had the power to burn me or suck me into hell.

He thought for a moment, rubbing his eyes.

Finally he said, "Jaqueline was a girl who was very important to your mother."

"So I'm about to understand, if I keep reading."

"You should keep reading."

"I will, but I want to know."

"She loved Jaqueline very much," my father said. "She wanted to validate her memory."

"So I have another girl's name."

He thought some more and finally said, "She considered it a great honor, to pass that name on to you."

"Well, what if I don't want some other girl's name?"

He shrugged and said, "It's why we decided to call you Lynne. You're not the same. It's a memory. It's an homage."

"Did the other Jaqueline contribute to my mother becoming a criminal?"

"You should keep reading," he said.

"Tell me this: Am I named after someone good or someone bad?"

"Someone very, very good," he said. "Who never had the opportunities that you have."

"So she never had a car."

He smiled at me. "She never even had a chance."

I decided to let it be. I went back to my room and went directly to sleep and didn't dream.

SIXTEEN
and Technically Three Days

• 1 •

I woke up around one a.m. and couldn't get back to sleep. I was staring at the ceiling as if it were a movie screen, watching all these characters I didn't know move around and play their parts. The strange girl with my name. My mother, who didn't really look like me (I had gotten my father's coloring; some people said I had her smile but I didn't see it), suddenly looked exactly like me in the movie. I was the one who was living in this crazy house with the distant smoking mother and the strange, fire-setting father. And now I had a new friend to think about. I couldn't wait until morning to find out about her. I turned on the bedside light and started to read again.

September 29

The girl's name was Jaqueline. She was a teenager. She was the oldest girl of a man who was a machinist in my father's carpet factory. He was divorced and had remarried a younger woman. They had children together, two girls, Dana and Sheryl, who were both roughly my age. They lived in the bad part of my neighborhood—the poor housing. We were allowed to play together, though my parents made it clear that they were beneath us in terms of social status. Jaqueline wasn't on anyone's social scale. She was just a wild teenager.

She tried to be good. She worked hard in school and made good grades. But when her parents weren't looking, which was most of the time, she was wild. She had a much older boyfriend who rode a motorcycle. She wore hot pants and smoked on the streets. When her long hair got in the way, she pulled it back and put on a bandanna. She smiled and laughed a lot. She had a good attitude.

Once when my father was driving home from work, he saw her standing outside a local gas station, in her short shorts, smoking a cigarette, and he said, "If I ever see my girls doing that, I will beat them until they can't sit down."

I didn't know what he was talking about.

Around this time, my mother had finally reached her limit in terms of living with my father and complying with his rules. My father was an important businessman in town; my mother should have help. My sister and I weren't much trouble, but we were children and she needed to be free to participate in the garden club and church functions. In order for her to do that, they needed help. They had gone through a couple of black women. My father had so much trouble accepting black help that he just canceled the whole thing. My mother was fed up. "I just need someone to look after the girls a few hours in the afternoon. A local girl to help out." Jaqueline was looking for work and her father was an employee. My father finally consented.

They hired Jaqueline to babysit occasionally and to clean up after us. My father decided to abandon his prejudice and to see it as helping out the lower class. Jaqueline, or Jackie as she was known to us, was the perfect solution. She enjoyed playing with me and my sister. She'd cook on the days my mother felt overwhelmed by the heat. She never complained. They paid her by the hour. It was all good.

Sandra and I loved being babysat by Jackie. She told us great stories about ghosts and aliens from other planets. She played card games with us and scared us silly with her worldview ("the world behind your eyes," she called it), to the point that we could barely sleep when she looked after us. But we loved her and our parents knew it. Her wild boyfriend with the motorcycle kept his distance, usually. Every now and then he'd stop by, but his involvement consisted of glasses of iced tea on the front porch. Though he often offered to take us for rides on his motorcycle, he never actually did it. His name was Lance and he had a shaved head and tattoos. Jackie stared at him with a quizzical expression, as if she were witnessing physics defined.

He had given her a bracelet that was the most beautiful thing I had ever seen. It was silver with birds on it. She used to let me play with it, even though she never took it off her wrist. She held it up and the birds encircled her wrist and I would inspect each one and give them names.

She'd say, "This is to remind me that no matter where you are, you can always fly away."

That was her plan with Lance. To fly away somewhere better. That was my plan, too, and maybe it still is. But it's getting harder and harder to believe in that idea.

I looked at the bracelet and I felt a chill pass through me. Now I had the girl's jewelry as well as her name. Where was this going to end?

Only one way to find out.

Jackie was like a cool older sister we had somehow inherited. Sandra liked to impress her and pretended they were peers. But I just looked up to her and listened and imitated her every move. I imagined myself having a boyfriend like Lance and riding on the back of his motorcycle. I imagined the bird bracelet on my arm and Jackie said she would give it to me when she finally decided to leave town.

"What if you forget?" I'd ask her.

"I won't forget."

"What if you leave in the middle of the night?"

"I'll know in advance. Getting out takes planning. Lance and I are working on it, but we're not going to just up and disappear."

"Are you sure?"

"I'm sure, little Cat."

Then she'd laugh and say, "But does that make sense? Giving my birds to a Cat? You're not going to eat them, are you?"

I assured her I wouldn't. I took the whole thing too seriously to laugh at her joke.

Every day I thought of Jackie and about when I'd see her again and what games we'd play. I never let on to Sandra or anybody how important she was to me. I was afraid they'd be jealous, and when people are jealous, they do desperate things.

But the problem wasn't about me and Jackie. The problem came from some dark place I couldn't have imagined.

There were arguments in my house. There were always arguments in my house, so many that I couldn't pay attention to them all. But these arguments I heard because, over and over, they were saying Jackie's name. My mother loved her at first and defended her, while my father argued against her. He said she was fast and trashy and was a bad influence on the girls. He said there were rumors about her around town. My mother said people in this town just talked for sport and it was none of their business who she hired to help out. She was finally getting some relief and he was just complaining because he didn't want her to have a life. Then it was back to how her people had money and they always had someone helping out and he just didn't know that because he grew up poor.

Then the roles changed. The shift happened slowly. First my father stopped complaining about Jackie. Then he started finding things to like about her. She was smarter than he thought, she was starting to dress better, she was good with the girls. He still hated her motorcycle boyfriend, but he suspected she was trying to make something of her life. It was fine if my mother wanted to keep her on.

Then my mother changed. Sometimes she did that just to spite him. That seemed to be the case again. There were loud fights in the living room after Jackie went home. My mother accused my father of being too interested in her. She said terrible things, like my father had a taste for trailer trash because that was where he came from. My father accused her of being crazy. Loud voices and eventually things being thrown. Sandra and I didn't know what to think. Selfishly I was hoping that if Jackie got fired, I'd still get the bracelet. And that maybe she would think of me and take me with her and Lance. We'd live on the road like a hippie family. We'd fly away to someplace where no one yelled or called people names or threw things. This was my dream.

One day my mother called me and Sandra into the living room and told us that Jackie wouldn't be coming around anymore. We were confused and upset. She told us to stop fretting about a babysitter, there were more babysitters in the world, we'd like the new one just fine. Sandra went with that idea but I threw a big fuss and got sent to my room. That same night, my father called us into the den and said, "Jackie is still going to be your babysitter."

"Why?" Sandra asked.

"Because I said so. And I'm still the last word in this family."

My mother sat in the kitchen smoking and drinking iced tea.

I was thrilled about the news but terrified to show it. I still remember my mother glaring at me as I walked past the kitchen. Or maybe I imagined it. That was how it always felt in my house, anyway. You had to take sides, and then someone was glaring at you.

Jackie kept coming and my mother ignored her and my father, oddly enough, was cold to her. She was caught in the middle of a battle that didn't seem to have anything to do with her. She was just a piece of land they were fighting over. Like the Civil War. My father had won, but he wasn't sure what to do with the victory.

One night, when Jackie was babysitting, my father came home early from his business meetings while my mother was still out with her friends. Sandra and I were supposed to be asleep but I always stayed awake until one of my parents came home. I heard raised voices and I got out of bed and crept downstairs. I hovered in the kitchen, which was just a few steps away from the den, where they were talking. I listened.

Jackie was saying this:

"I don't care if I work for you or not, but I know what I know."

Daddy was saying this:

"Jackie, I can see you want a better life for yourself. I understand that, I do. I want to see that happen for you."

"Ha, like you care about me."

"Of course I care about you. I don't want you to do anything unwise."

Jackie said, "I can't forget what I know."

"You're a very young girl. Your thinking can be confused."

"I'm not confused."

Daddy said, "Jackie, I don't want anything bad to happen to you."

She said, "I'm not scared of you."

"Of course you're not. Why would I want you to be?"

She said, "You think you own this town. You think you have people fooled."

"Why would I want to fool people?"

"I'm not an idiot. I pick up on things."

"Of course you do."

"And those girls, they're going to figure it out."

"Let's leave the girls out of it."

"I can't. They're in it. Your wife is smarter than you think, too."

"Jackie, I'm wondering if the stress of your life is getting to you. Going to school, working all these hours, having a boyfriend. And the way people talk about you . . . that has to be difficult."

"Talk about *me*? I'm not the one who should be worried about talk."

He began mumbling and then she mumbled back and I exhausted my hearing. All I could understand was the intensity of their discussion, rumbling like an underground railroad.

Then she left.

I saw her alive only once more.

It was a couple of weeks before Christmas. My father said he was going to cut down a Christmas tree. We never bought a tree. Why would we? We lived near a forest, and in those days, you could just walk out into it and bring home a tree.

My father was about to embark on this journey to cut down a tree and I wanted to go with him. I was his sidekick, after all. He always took me everywhere. When I said I wanted to go, he couldn't resist. My mother dressed me up in my new winter coat and my new winter hat, a furry pixie deal with a pointed top. I got in the truck with my father and we went to get the tree.

I rode in the truck next to my father, in my new winter clothes. We listened to Christmas songs on the radio. He parked next to the edge of the woods. The heater was blasting and I was starting to sweat. He shut off the engine and turned to me. I can still see him, slipping on his work gloves and adjusting his black wool cap.

He said, "I'm going to chop down the tree. You should wait here."

"I thought I was going with you."

"You are with me," he said, with a smile. He had a nice smile. He made me feel important.

"But I want to help you with the tree."

"You'll just get cold out there. I'll be back in a few minutes."

It didn't make much sense, as I was all dressed up in my winter gear, but I agreed. I would have done anything to make my father happy. He always seemed so smart and in charge. I knew he had his bad moments. He had a mean streak and he yelled. But I had a strong sense that he held things together in my family. I had a sense he was in charge.

I was his idea, which meant that I was not allowed to disappoint him. If I disappointed him, I would be left alone with my mother, who never wanted me.

"It'll be okay, Cat," he said. "Just wait here."

He got out of the truck and I turned around to watch him. He went to the back and got out an ax and some rope and a big piece of plastic. He flashed a smile at me as he walked by. I watched him disappear into the woods.

A long time seemed to pass. Although it was cold, the winter sun was persistent and as it shone into the truck, I started to get hot. I tried to get out of my new winter gear but my mother had knotted the strings on the hat and buttoned my coat so securely that I felt I was trapped in some kind of puzzle. I managed to get my mittens off, but I was still hot. I got out of the truck and went to look for him.

I went into the woods feeling confident. After all, these were the same woods that my friends and I played in. I knew them like the back of my hand. I could point out the bicycle tire tracks we had made, the pretend houses we had built, the landmarks we had created with rocks and trees. But as I stumbled down the hill, everything looked unfamiliar to me. I wasn't with my friends anymore and suddenly the woods looked dense and scary. The air outside was much colder than it had been in the truck, and I regretted taking off my mittens. My fingers were white with cold and every branch I touched stung them.

I thought of Hansel and Gretel walking through the woods, leaving bread crumbs. Suddenly I wasn't sure I could find my way back to the truck. I had been sure I'd see my father right away, but all I saw were tree trunks and I heard nothing but hollow sounds, the leaves shivering, the few remaining winter birds making desperate chirps.

I saw some bushes shaking in the distance. I followed the shaking.

I was relieved because I knew the shaking bushes meant a person was around. It had to be my father. He had found a tree and was chopping it down. I could help.

"Daddy," I said.

No answer.

"Daddy," I yelled.

Still, no answer. I moved through the brush. I felt briars catching my clothes.

I came into a clearing.

I saw my father and I was relieved. I had found him.

There he was. He was yards away from me. I saw his dark coat and his dark cap and his work gloves.

The ax and the rope and the bag were on the ground beside him.

I saw him wrestling a tree. He was struggling with it. He was choking it, as if the tree could fight back.

But it wasn't a tree.

It was Jackie.

I stood and I stared and I tried to make sense of it.

We went to get a Christmas tree.

His hands were around her throat.

I thought, Is she helping us get the tree?

I thought, Is he joking? Are they kidding around?

She saw me. Her arm reached out. The birds were

around it. They danced. It was like she was trying to hold my hand. I reached toward her, too, but nothing happened.

She looked at me, as if to say "Save me."

He was killing her.

The birds. The birds.

Then my father saw me.

I looked at him and he looked at me.

The birds on her wrist made a singing noise.

I turned and ran.

I ran up the hill as fast as I could. The mud made a slurping sound underneath my feet. The briars grabbed at me. Something in my head told me to go back, and something else in my head said, Run as fast as you can. I couldn't run fast. A limb caught my hat and pulled it off. I grabbed it back and then I kept running.

I thought I was next.

I ran until I could see the truck at the edge of the woods. Then I felt some force around my waist. My father had reached me. He picked me up.

"I told you to stay in the truck," he said.

"I . . . I was hot."

"When are you going to learn?" he asked me.

"I don't know."

"Do what I tell you to do."

"I'm going to the truck."

"No," he said.

He set me down on the ground and I looked at him. Sweat was trickling down his face. He wiped it away, still wearing his work gloves.

He sighed and looked to the sky.

He said, "It's too late. You have to help me now."

"I'll help you," I said.

He said, "You don't understand."

I knew I didn't understand. But I didn't know what to say.

This was my father. This was Jackie. They had some secret understanding. I had interfered.

I don't know what happened next. Maybe we stood next to the edge of the woods for a while, talking.

Imagine my whole world crashing down. I thought back to my mother, dressing me in my new winter wear. I thought back to meeting Jackie, to her promising me the bird bracelet.

I couldn't stop crying.

He calmed me down somehow. He said a million things, probably. He said, "Your mother is crazy and your sister is sick and you were my idea." He said, "Trust me, don't worry, this is what we have to do."

He said, "Come back here with me."

And I knew nothing then of history. He was just my father.

Everything that happened next is unclear.

I think we walked back to where I saw him wrestling with a tree. I think her body was lying there. I think she was faceup to the cold winter sun and she looked just like I remembered her, except that her face was frozen in a stunned expression.

I think he said, "She was not a good person."

97

I think I abandoned my idea of her. I think I chose my father in that moment.

She was lifeless. We dragged her body into the truck. Then we drove the truck to another part of the forest. He was quiet the whole time. I made a decision not to speak. Every now and then I glanced at her and I saw the bird bracelet dangling. I wanted to touch it but didn't.

I saw her red hair spilling across her chest and I wanted to touch that, too, but I didn't move.

After we parked again, I helped him take her out of the car. We carried her into the woods. We approached an abandoned well—they were all over and I had been warned against playing near them. I saw the well and I was scared because he had done such a good job of warning me away from such a place. I saw the disorganized pieces of lumber in the middle of the woods and I knew that a dark, forever place lay beneath them.

I think this really happened because I remember holding her by the wrist. I remember looking at the bird bracelet.

We dragged her toward the well and she got stuck on some rocks and a shoe came off. I don't know what happened then. The bracelet was still digging into my palm. I unhooked it and slipped it into my pocket.

It seemed like a lot of time passed.

He told me to go sit on a rock and watch for intruders. I did that. I wasn't sure what I was looking for. I had played enough in the woods to know that no grown-ups ever came there.

When it was taking too long I walked back to the well. I

saw him leaning over it and he stood up and said, "What did I tell you to do?"

I went back to the rock and watched. No one came.

Finally he came and found me. He looked tired. He touched my hair. He said, "Hey, are you okay?"

I didn't know what to say.

He said, "Let's go home. You need a snack or something."

Then we drove back home.

Right before we pulled up at the house, he turned to me and said, "What's good about you and me is that we have our own language. Right? We understand each other. You're my idea."

I can't remember what I said.

My mother met us outside. "What have you been doing?" she asked. "Where's the tree?"

"We couldn't find a good tree," he said.

"What do you mean you couldn't find a tree?" she asked.

"I think we might have to go to a lot this year," he said, dusting off the arms of his jacket.

"But you were gone so long," my mother said.

"We were looking. There was nothing."

My mother turned her eyes on me. She was beautiful and nervous. Her eyes were black and quick. There was nowhere to hide.

I looked at my father.

"What happened to her?" she asked, looking at me and my frayed clothing.

I already couldn't remember. I had no idea that my

clothes were torn and dirty. My mittens were gone, my pixie hat was chewed up, my winter coat was full of briar scratches. I just stared at my mother.

My father said, "We were in the woods. We were looking. Give us a break."

That night he came to my room and read me the Bible passage in which God asks Abraham to kill his only son, Isaac. He read the passage to me and explained that sometimes it's okay for parents to kill their children.

After he left, I lay in bed and held the bracelet and I talked to Jackie.

When I woke up the next morning, I was sure it had all been a dream.

A week later, there was a search party. The gossip was that Jackie had run away with her no-good motorcycle-riding boyfriend. But the boyfriend showed up, all concerned about her absence. So the search party took place. While my parents were searching in the woods for her, I was in the basement with her sisters, Dana and Sheryl. Jackie was gone and no one knew why, but I knew why. I sat in the basement and knew why.

While I was playing cards, you and your brother came into the room. I know you don't remember this. And it took me a long time to remember it, too, but now I'm certain. Your brother was taller and his hair and eyes were lighter, and he had this confident way about him. You were shorter and quieter and you sort of hung back. I remember our eyes connecting.

Someone in the room asked who you were and no one

had an immediate answer. We all knew you didn't live in Union Grade.

Then someone said, "They're her cousins."

Someone else said, "She doesn't have cousins."

Someone else said, "That's just what I heard."

I didn't pay that much attention to you. I'll be honest about that. I mainly registered your face because you were a stranger to our town. I didn't encounter that many strangers. It took me a long time to make the connection. I didn't make it the first day I saw you again, this fall, at Union Grade High. I didn't make it the second or the third time. It was when people started to gossip and I heard the story. I remembered being in that basement and I remembered seeing you and it all fell into place.

But that day in the basement of Jackie's house, I wasn't thinking about you. I was thinking of the bird bracelet. I knew it was my one link to what was happening and I was worried about someone finding it.

I had put it behind a loose board in my closet, where I'm currently hiding this letter in between writing it. It's all I have left of her, and all I really have of my experience that night. Whenever I start to think it didn't happen, I take the bracelet out and hold it.

Holding it has been like holding my own sanity.

Lately, seeing you has reminded me of my sanity all over again. I know it happened just as I remember it.

For a lot of years after that, I woke up in the middle of the night, scared to death and longing to answer for something I had done. Sometimes I honestly couldn't remember what it was. But most times I remembered as if I were watching the movie and it was all happening again.

I became a criminal that day in the woods.

I am telling you now so you won't make the mistake of falling in love with me.

This is who I am.

Do you still want to date me? I didn't think so.

So just stop staring at me in English class and trying to talk to me and hoping to get to know me.

If you even think about loving me, remember who I am. I'm telling you for your own good. My own good is a thing of the past. It's a kind of slight memory I have, of smelling breakfast when I wake up and thinking I'll go down and greet my family and they will be all good and normal. That's over for me.

No reason it should be over for you.

• 2 •

I sat at the kitchen table in the dark.

The manuscript was in front of me.

It was two o'clock in the morning.

I stared at the letter. I stared at the bird bracelet sitting next to it. I was thinking of lighting the paper on fire and throwing the bracelet on top. I didn't know what to do. So far that was my only idea.

Then I had another idea. I decided to light a candle. Then I took a framed picture of my mother that usually sat on the coffee table and I put it next to the manuscript and the bracelet, and the whole thing looked like a sacrifice of some kind, ready to make its way toward heaven, where my mother may or may not have been, depending on what you believe or I believed or the president believed or the latest big celebrity believed on any given day.

Me, I was admitting to total confusion. I was giving in to it.

And I was sitting next to this homemade halfhearted offering and I wasn't moving. I was just staring.

My grandfather was a murderer. He killed a girl with his bare hands. My mother saw it. She never told anyone. Except Noah.

Then she died.

This would make a nice essay on my college application.

Or a nice opening paragraph on my first date.

I knew all about DNA. They taught it in school. Made a big deal of it. You are your DNA. Genetic memory.

The stairs creaked.

My father came downstairs, as I knew he would.

He was wearing his pajama bottoms and a white T-shirt and his hair was all over the place and his reading glasses were far down his nose and he looked concerned.

"Lynnie?" he said.

"Jaqueline," I answered.

He sighed and sat across the table from me and ran his fingers through his hair.

"You're not going to insist on being called that, are you?"

"Why? Would it bother you?"

"I'm too old to call you another name."

"Is that it?"

"You know it isn't. Lynne is what your mother and I agreed to call you. It was our agreement."

"It's my name."

"Yes, it is."

I waited for a long moment, letting the time settle down on him like ash, and I enjoyed his discomfort. I was mad at him and I wanted him to know why before I said it.

"When were you going to tell me the truth?"

He seemed surprised. "I did. By giving you the letter. And the bracelet. You weren't ready before."

"That's not what I'm talking about."

He stared at me. I took a breath and wondered if I should bring the whole house down now or save it for later, for when I needed something. But I realized that I was done with all the mystery and the game playing and the whole sorry history of not knowing and not talking about it.

"You're Noah, aren't you?"

He took his glasses off and folded them and then he clasped his fingers and put them under his chin.

"Yes, I am."

I shook my head and looked away. I felt in control. The next move was mine. And the next and the next. I sat there wondering what to do with all that power. He sat across from me, my strong father with all the answers, and he didn't know what to do.

"Why?" I asked.

"Why what?"

"Why did she call you that?"

This question actually made him smile and then my eyes met his and he wanted me to smile with him and I refused.

He said, "When I first moved there, nobody knew my name. I was shy and I didn't make friends right away. I stared at your mother a lot. The first time I saw her I was smitten. I wanted to talk to her but I didn't know how. She noticed it right away. She wanted a name for me but she didn't know how to ask. So she decided my name was Noah. Because I had this long hair, like someone from the Bible, she said, and because girls followed me around in twos, like animals following Noah to the ark."

I didn't respond. I just listened.

His mind was wandering, anyway. I wondered if he even knew I was there anymore.

"She thought I didn't know about the nickname but I did. I liked it. Noah seemed like a much more interesting name than John. Noah sounded like a rock star or a private-school boy or someone who was going places. I just let it happen."

I waited.

He smiled some more. He said, "Your mother. She was so beautiful. Not in a way that was trying, you see. She didn't wear makeup, and her hair just hung down to her waist, parted in the middle, and she had these great eyes and she was always wearing jeans. But it was her smile, really. It lit up her whole face. Your mother had a way of making me feel that everything was going to be fine. Later, when I knew the whole story, I was so surprised by that. She had lived through all this trouble. But she still believed the world was a good place to be and there was something to hope for. No reason for her to think that. It was something that was in her."

I gave that a moment to sink in. I always wanted to hear about my mother. But I was mad at him and I didn't want to make him feel better by being entertained.

After a respectable amount of time had passed, I asked, "Who was Jackie to you?"

He wasn't surprised by the question.

"She was my cousin."

"Did you know her?"

He shook his head.

"I had heard about her for years, of course. After the accident. That's what we called it in my family. I'm not sure why. There was never an accident. My mother always understood that. There was a disappearance. An incident. But calling it that left things so wide open. Calling it an accident meant that it was over. My father insisted on it. He wanted my mother to understand it was over."

I waited.

He looked at me. "Wait, I want to be honest. I did know her. Apparently I met her on several occasions. Christmases and family reunions. But I was much younger. Six or seven years younger. I don't remember her at all. Your mother knew her much better."

I waited for more. I saw him shifting in his chair. He wanted to go back to bed.

Still I waited.

He said, "Lynne, I'm glad you know all this. I think I did the right thing. Sometimes it's hard for me to know. I need guidance from your mother but I don't have that anymore. So I'm just winging it. The hard part is over now, though. You've read the letter. I've been waiting for that moment my whole adult life. Now I think we can move forward and get things accomplished."

"What things?"

He shrugged. "It's going to be the truth from now on."

"Oh, really, is that how it's going to be?"

He nodded. He stood. He pushed his chair in.

"We should go to bed. It's late."

I shook my head at him.

"I want to hear the rest."

My father looked at me, completely caught in the net, the battle plan unraveling in front of him.

"It's late, Lynnie."

"You gave me the letter. You can't leave me alone with it now. You think I'm going to go upstairs and set my alarm and go to bed and get up for school as usual?"

I could see he did think that. Or more accurately, he hadn't thought past this point.

"Lynnie, we have obligations."

"You wanted me to read the letter. I've read it. Now I have some questions, Dad. And we'll stay up all night if we have to."

My father was not the kind of man you could boss around. I saw his shoulders hunching up and his facial features collecting in the middle. But I wasn't afraid. I hadn't asked for the letter. Or the bracelet. I had asked for a car.

I could see his resolve was weakening and I waited. He tried once again.

He said, "This could take all night."

"Okay," I said.

He thought about it and sat back down. The candle was flickering between us and the letter was between us and we had reached a crossroads. He had always known this day was coming and I had never known. But now I did and I had to know more.

So he began talking. He told me the story. Not as he was—a grown man, a widower, with a teenage daughter and a job in a law firm and a house and a car and a college fund and obligations, as he put it, and places to be and people to see and a whole made-up life to attend to. He told me the story as he experienced it then. Just a boy, a little younger than me, who moved to a small town and met a pretty girl with long hair parted in the middle and a smile he couldn't forget. It was there that he met his past and his future and it all came together and fell apart and eventually turned into me.

• 3 •

We were a happy family. Everybody thinks they are. Everybody assumes they are. Nobody asks questions. I had no reason to ask any. We lived in Manhattan. East Side. My father was a dentist. My mother was a housewife. She was a little nervous—that's the worst that can be said of her during that time. My older brother, Charlie, was a star athlete. He was five years older than I was and he might as well have been twenty. I adored him and I hung around him and tried to be like him, but he had plans and commitments. My parents put all their hopes in him. There was never any question of him being anything but spectacular. While other families sat around at night and watched TV, we just watched Charlie.

We watched him mimic his friends or recount his athletic stunts of the day, and I was quiet, watching and waiting to prove myself.

There wasn't much in the way of extended family. My father's parents had come over from Italy and had died young. All we had left of them was their surname. My father couldn't remember what they had expected of him other than to live in America and become a success. He had achieved that. The youngest of some sprawling immigrant family, he felt cut loose.

They didn't care who he married. No one was watching or holding him accountable. He met her in a restaurant; she was his waitress. He told me he fell in love with her before she ever spoke a word and I dreamed of falling in love with some woman that way, and eventually I did.

Her name was Ella and that was an exotic-sounding name to him because he'd never met anyone from the South. Growing up in Brooklyn he was surrounded by Mary Catherines and Mary Louises and Mary Theresas and just plain Marys. Ella wasn't a saint at all. Ella was from somewhere else, and she spoke slowly and with an accent and her manner calmed him down. And for some reason she was in Manhattan, the Lower East Side.

Ella was displaced. She had run away from home, a place called Union Grade. She missed her family, but she had vowed never to go back to the place. She didn't say why, but he knew. They were poor. It was the South. There was probably a trailer involved and a bad uncle and maybe even a bad father or something she was running away from that chased her for a while but wouldn't go as far north as Manhattan. She had left behind a sister, a younger sister, the only one she really talked about. Her name was Charlene. Ella missed her and worried about her all the time, but she couldn't risk going back for her. Charlene was a beauty, she said, with auburn hair and blue eyes and bone china skin.

My dad started dental school and Ella, my mother, kept

working as a waitress and eventually they got married. Dad scraped together enough money to send a bus ticket to Charlene. She came out and stayed with them and she was beautiful and quiet and sad and damaged. Ella was happy to have her little sister with her, but there was something broken about her and they couldn't fix it. There was something broken like that in my mother, too, but it took a while to come out. It hovered like a ghost most of the time and she was all right.

Charlene got pregnant that summer in New York. She went back home without telling anybody who or what or where. She went back to Union Grade and made up a story about a husband in New York and had the baby and named her Jaqueline.

A year after Charlene went back home my mother had my older brother and named him Charles, after her sister with the auburn hair and the sad eyes. I think she always felt responsible for what happened to Charlene in the city. They tried to keep an eye on her, but they didn't do a very good job. Nobody ever knew who the father was. This isn't a Tennessee Williams story, so it wasn't my father. It was just some sailor, my mom told me. Some guy she remembered seeing Charlene with, sitting on the stoop near their apartment in Brooklyn. But he disappeared into the ocean like some character in a Puccini opera, and Charlene went back home.

Around the time Charlie was born, Charlene met a machinst in Union Grade named Bo Rivers and he was good to her and married her and later they had two more daughters, Dana and Sheryl. Baby Jackie had a father and Charlene was settled and that gave my mother some peace of mind.

So the story had a happy middle. Not so much a happy ending.

My mother finally felt brave enough to go back down South to Union Grade, taking Charlie with her. Her parents were dead by then and she'd been gone long enough that nobody thought of her as trailer trash. They thought of her as the dentist's wife from Manhattan, which was an odd thing to be but perfectly respectable. It was good for her to see Charlene doing so well, and Ella fell in love with Baby Jackie right away.

The way she told it, Charlie and Baby Jackie looked alike. They could have been brother and sister. Charlie had red hair then. It turned dark later. But they always shared the blue eyes. I wasn't born yet. I wasn't even an idea.

They stayed in touch over the years and Ella had me and I was dark like my dad and reminded her of nobody from Union Grade, so she treated me like a stranger, one she was delighted to raise, but who had nothing whatsoever to do with her. To be fair, the brokenness was kicking in around that time. Those weren't bad memories, though. My mother just seemed distant but happy and all I cared about was following Charlie around.

When Charlie was fifteen and I was ten, Baby Jackie disappeared.

She wasn't a baby then, of course. She was older than both of us. Charlie and I called her Cousin Jackie but Mom still called her Baby because that was the way she remembered her. It was funny, we didn't talk about the other cousins at all. Dana and Sheryl, the two girls she had with Bo Rivers the machinist. They were younger than us, so we didn't care. But Jackie was different to us because she was different to my mother. She was her special niece, like the daughter she never had, like the sister she felt she hadn't taken care of.

So it hit her hard when Baby Jackie went missing.

It was late in the game by the time my parents found out. Charlene and Bo took three days to even report it, which made my mother angry, but Charlene explained. "She has a boyfriend. She's always running off with him."

"For three days?" my mother asked, shrieking on the phone in our living room. Charlie and I sat on our baseball mitts and listened.

"A day once," Charlene had said. "She ran away because we wouldn't let her wear hip-huggers to school."

"But three days," my mother insisted, pacing in our living room and smoking. Her hair was unbrushed and her eyes looked wild. "Did you call the police?"

Charlene said there was no point.

"No point? No point? How do you people live?"

When she hung up the phone she looked at us as if we were the problem and said, "She never knew how to take care of herself, let alone a baby."

I remember Charlie said, "Jackie's older than me, Mom."

"That's not the point. My God, what *is* your point, Charles?"

That's how upset she was. She was not only yelling at Charlie, she was calling him Charles. I was usually the one in trouble.

Charlie talked to her the way Dad did, so he was condescending. Even calling her by her first name. "My point, Ella, is that she's old enough to take care of herself."

112

"Oh, is that what you think? I suppose that's what you both think. Well, let me tell you something you might have missed along the way. She's a girl. Girls are different. Girls are not safe in this world. Girls are exposed."

She stopped talking and started crying into her fingers and then she left the room.

Charlie and I didn't say anything because we were afraid of what we had just seen. Charlie was unsettled because he was seeing the future. Our mother was starting to come apart.

I was seeing the past. Whatever it was that made her that way.

So that was that and we were heading down South. Her favorite niece was missing and she was going to save her the way she couldn't save Charlene—at least, that's what was in her head.

They took us out of school and we went down to Union Grade to be part of the search party. To Charlie and me it was a kind of adventure, a chance to get out of school. I was sure they were going to find her so there wasn't any urgency and nothing much to worry about except the frantic way my mother was behaving and how she kept forgetting to brush her hair or put on makeup.

Did I meet your mother on that trip? I know that's what you're thinking and I don't have an answer. We argued about it. She said yes, she remembered seeing me. I said no, I would have remembered seeing her. She said she looked a lot different. She was only a little kid. I guess we both were, but it felt like I was old. I guess it felt like that to her, too. Which was why she felt so guilty all those years.

We were so little. We were so incapable of doing anything

much. But your consciousness, it always feels big, doesn't it? It always feels exactly the same.

Anyway, she wasn't part of the search party. She was in the basement playing cards with the younger kids and she said I came into the basement with Charlie, but I don't remember it. She said she remembered it because her sister Sandra was there and she immediately got a crush on Charlie and wouldn't stop talking about it.

There's no point arguing about it. It's strange enough that we were so close to each other. And neither of us knew that we were going to meet soon, that I was going to move there and our lives were going to be forever changed because of what was happening that weekend.

She told me that she was sitting in the basement feeling a vague sense of dread, something like a stomach flu, and she didn't know why and she did. She knew what she knew but it was all fading, she said, like a dream, and she couldn't tell the real parts from the unreal parts and decided to make up her own reality. Later she put me into that reality because she liked it better that way.

We didn't find Jackie and the police didn't find her; nobody found her.

We sat in my aunt Charlene's house and she cried and drank and my mother tried to take her drinks away. Dad and that guy Bo sat in the kitchen and talked in low voices and wrote things down on pieces of paper. Charlie and I watched TV and pitched a football around in the yard. That's all I remember.

Except on the way home my mother looked crazy and she

didn't eat anything and she started chain-smoking. Dad would take the cigarettes out of her hand and she would just light another one. Eventually he gave up.

After that, nothing was the same.

Charlie went off to college and that made my mother even worse. She stopped getting dressed until around dinnertime and then she made me and Dad frozen meals in the microwave, and when he complained she told him there was no point in cooking for three people. Dad looked at me and said, "John's still here, Ella, and we're still a family."

"You have a family," she would say to him. "Mine's all gone."

That didn't make me feel great. But I was a boy turning into a man and I had to act like it didn't matter. I started hanging out on the streets of Manhattan with my friends, and we'd get into innocuous kinds of trouble—shoplifting and throwing firecrackers into the East River and trying to run over tourists with our skateboards in the park. We rode the subway from one end to the other and we snuck into bars and we tried to pick up French girls in museums and we rode the Roosevelt Island tram for no reason and we'd hang out on the island for no reason and pretend we had run away from home.

Then my friends had to go home. But I never had to go home. My mother didn't know what time it was and she didn't care.

When I turned fourteen my father had had enough. I was already getting suspended from school and my grades were dropping and my mother never left the living room of our apartment. He decided only a move could save us. Only a move to Union Grade.

• 4 •

I saw your mother almost as soon as we landed. Our house was across town from where they lived. We were in a neat little housing development called Pinewood Park (even though there were no pines and no park) and she lived on Carter Street, near the town, in one of the many Victorian mansions. Though the houses were big there, the whole area was in a state of slow decay. It was where the up-and-coming moved to make their mark, or where the ancestors of the rich stayed, trying to keep up appearances. The really well-to-do people lived in Pinewood Park. A division was created. My father was a wealthy professional and hers was a self-made man trying to prove himself.

It was almost impossible to live in Union Grade and not know who her father was. He was on the town council and he was a prominent businessman and he was a deacon in the church. He was well-respected, but there was an aura of, what do you call it, otherness about him. He was a powerful person in the town, but everyone regarded him with a certain degree of suspicion. There were rumors about him. He had made it big by making certain deals with the devil. Nobody knew what those deals were. Nobody cared. He had established himself and everyone had to contend with him.

The area where they lived bordered the poor part of town, and that was where Jackie and her family had once lived. By the time we arrived, Jackie's family had moved away, leaving no forwarding address. My father had talked my mother into moving there with the vague promise that maybe we would find them all again. At the very least, we would be nearby in case Jackie should ever resurface. He knew she wasn't going to come back. He knew she was gone. But he held this promise out to my mother because he wanted to save her, and he knew nothing else could reach her. So he moved her to Union Grade and she lived there with the porch light on, waiting, like a crazed widow who leaves the light on for her husband killed in the war. Everyone knew but Mom, and Dad used her unwillingness to know against her. Or maybe for her. He only wanted her to be normal again.

I went along because there was nothing else for me to do and I missed Charlie. He was at the University of North Carolina in Chapel Hill, playing football and baseball for them, and he kept in touch because he liked us well enough, but we all knew he had left. He was on his journey to greatness. He got married right out of college to a girl named Lane. I only met her a couple of times, once at their wedding. They both went on to become landscape architects and now they travel the world designing the grounds for major resorts. They never had children that I know of. I've lost touch. I lost them when I lost the rest of my family, but I'm getting ahead of myself.

Back to your mother. I saw her the first day I went to town. I rode my bike in at Ella's request. She told me she needed some time to unpack and I should go ahead and check out the place and try to make some friends. I took my ten-speed into town and locked it to a meter and walked around. I went into the drugstore and I saw a small pack of girls sitting at the counter, eating french fries and drinking Cokes. They were all pretty, but your mother was the prettiest. Partly because she wasn't trying. The other girls were all made-up and flirtatious; your mother was plain and unapologetic. They all glanced at me as I wandered around, pretending to be interested in, I don't know, magazines and batteries. I was dressing like New York back then, with my long hair and my hats and my torn jeans and my woven leather bracelets. I think I had an earring. She said I did but I don't remember that. All I remember is that when your mother looked at me our eyes locked and she smiled, this openmouthed kind of smile, as if she were surprised to see me again. Maybe she really did remember me from the search party. Or maybe she saw me the way I saw her. Just as my dad described seeing my mother. Oh, I thought, there she is. I'm going to marry her. And then she looked away.

When school started I looked for her. I couldn't find her in the halls, but to my great delight we had English class together. I used to sit in the back of the room and watch her, willing her to look at me, and sometimes she did. She was always writing in a spiral notebook. At first I thought she was taking down what the teacher said. Much later I realized she was writing the letter. But I knew, without knowing, that she was paying attention to me even when she turned her back, and I wanted to know what it was about.

A couple of times, leaving class, I tried to start a conversation with her, and even though her expression was warm and I could tell she liked me, she avoided talking to me and went for days pretending as if I didn't exist. I befriended Jimmy English, a boy she had known since she was little, hoping to get some information about her. Jimmy was understandably protective toward her, but I had P.E. class with him and I remember showing off, running as fast as I could, being the only guy who could climb the rope to the top of the gym, just so he would go back and tell her. Which he did. It made me happy to see that part in the letter.

I didn't try very hard to make friends. What your mother said was accurate. The girls were intrigued by me, but I paid them no mind, and the boys circled me with curiosity and agitation, and I eventually made friends with some of them by making the track team and trying out for baseball. (I was the relief pitcher. I wasn't any good. Looking back, I realized I didn't want to surpass Charlie, not that there was ever any chance of that.) When I realized your mother wasn't going to date me and I wasn't going to be the kind of athlete Charlie was, I focused on schoolwork. I had to. I wasn't going to spend my life in Union Grade. My mother was going crazier by the minute and my father was struggling to make it all okay, and I knew that if I didn't get busy, I'd be in that place for the rest of my life.

I didn't hate Union Grade. I didn't like it, either. I just didn't understand it. Here I was, a kid who had spent most of his adolescence running around the streets of Manhattan. Now I was confined to this pseudo-Colonial monstrosity in a gated community, where everyone's lawns and cars and basic floor plans were the same. We couldn't get noticed. We didn't want to get noticed. My mother didn't want anyone to know her connection to the place. No one remembered her and she liked it that way. Every now and then she'd leave the house and go to the grocery store or even attempt to join something like the garden club, and she would overhear the talk of the girl who disappeared so long ago, that wild girl Jackie, and she would hear the rumors of her being a hooker in Richmond or being a famous movie star or being dead. She never offered an opinion and she never revealed who she was. She just listened.

No one, including my father, knew what I knew in those days. My mother had lost her basic connection to planet Earth. I would come home in the afternoons and she would be sitting in the kitchen in front of a fan, even though we had air-conditioning, wearing a slip and smoking cigarettes and listening to the radio. She would look at me when I walked in and say, in her melancholy way, "Oh, look at you, you're so handsome."

And I would go to my room and she wouldn't talk to me again until dinner.

Sometimes during dinner, while my father was talking about his patients or about the new health clinic that was opening, or the block party they should probably attend, my mother would suddenly get a dose of consciousness and say, "Daddy, this is where I grew up. I know this place. Why are we here, Ray?"

My father's name was Ray. My mother didn't always remember it. Sometimes she would call him Charles or John and he would answer to anything she called him. He just loved her and he was eager for her to hold on to something, anything, that was remotely real.

Because of my isolation I kept studying and I started to get good grades and my mother decided I would be a lawyer. She would say, "Just think of it, John. If you became a lawyer you could solve Baby Jackie's disappearance."

My father would say, "It's fine for John to be a lawyer, Ella. But no one is going to find Jackie. Jackie is gone."

"I didn't say find her. I said solve her disappearance."

She would smoke and roll her eyes at him. My father would look at me, seeking out a partner, someone who might under-stand. I understood but I didn't want to. I just wanted the chance to be a normal teenager. Long before I read the letter, I knew your mom and I shared that connection. We just wanted to be normal, and circumstances were conspiring against us.

Maybe it was because Ella said the word *lawyer* to me. Or maybe it was because I sensed their loss and their frustration over never having found Jackie. And maybe it was that Jackie's family had been run out of town because of their loss, because of their low stature, and maybe their daughter had gone miss-ing precisely because she could, because no one else on earth felt obligated to find her . . . maybe it was for all those reasons that I became obsessed with a sense of justice. But I knew I was going to be a lawyer. I was going to be on the right side of the law. I was going to be the person who solved the puzzle that was left unsolved.

But that was a long time in the future. In the meantime, I was just the guy at the back of Ms. McKeever's English class who stared at a girl named Cat and drew pictures of her and dreamed.

Your mother gave me the letter in February. On Valentine's Day in fact. I'll tell you how it all went down. But something else happened first.

It was right after Christmas. Our first Christmas in Union Grade was odd and uneventful in the conventional sense. My father's family was dead and Charlie was in Taiwan with Lane on a semester abroad, and my mother had no idea where any of her family was. Still, we had to put together a Christmas. I had finished final exams and was tired and wanted to spend my vacation staring at the walls and listening to music. My parents decided they needed to explore the party circuit. My father thought networking would help him build his practice. So he dragged my mother out to a couple of parties on Christmas Eve. I was happy to see them go, happy to see them making a run at a life, and happy to see my mother come down the stairs in a nice black dress with her Tiffany pearls and high heels. She was always funny, my mother, even when she was crazy. And while she was waiting for my father to get ready she sat in the living room and smoked a cigarette and I sat beside her.

She said, "Dear God, John, your poor father thought he was fixing it for me by moving me to Union Grade. I hate this place. I spent my whole life trying to escape it."

"It's not so bad," I assured her.

She winked at me and said, "You've met a girl, haven't you?"

I didn't admit I had. To be honest, I hadn't really met your mother. I was just admiring her from the back of the room.

"Well, yeah, there's a girl."

"Who?" she asked.

Ordinarily, a guy my age wouldn't admit a crush if he were under torture. But because my mother was making an attempt to be normal, I wanted to meet her halfway. I said her name was Catherine. Catherine what? Pittman, I said.

My mother squinted and said, "Pittman."

"Yes."

She said, "Is her father Clyde Pittman?"

I didn't know.

She said, "He's on the town council. He's a big man in Union Grade."

"Oh," I said.

She smoked her cigarette and thought and she didn't say anything else.

They left and I probably watched TV and stole some of my mother's cigarettes and pretended to be a hockey player in the living room. I went to bed before midnight and the next thing I knew, my mother was sitting on the edge of my bed. I woke up and saw her sitting there, still in her black dress and pearls, looking past me to the window behind my bed. I sat up.

"Mother, are you okay?"

She nodded and sighed.

"What happened? Did you meet people?"

"We met people," she said.

"And you had a good time?"

She nodded and sighed.

I waited.

She said, "I talked to a woman who knew Jackie. It was Catherine Pittman's mother. A nice lady, I can't remember her first name. She said she was part of the search party. She said Jackie worked for them for a while. She loved her like a daughter, she said. Her whole family was broken up when Jackie ran away. Ran away, she said. I suggested that Jackie didn't run away, that she was hurt or even killed. But that nice lady said to me, no, everyone looked for her and she was long gone. Maybe she really did run away, John. Maybe all this time I've been thinking she was dead. But she's really alive and we're not wrong to wait."

I didn't say anything.

That was when I first heard the connection between your mom's parents and mine. I didn't know what to make of it. To be honest, I was a selfish boy and I was just hoping that this connection that her parents made with mine meant that Cat and I would meet. We would meet and chat and become friends and I could convince her that I was going to marry her because it was stuck in my mind.

My mother improved after that. She got up every day and dressed and went out and even joined some clubs. She had coffee with Cat's mother and she joined a bridge club and a swimming club, and soon she was part of Union Grade and she couldn't even remember Manhattan anymore. My father was pleased. My mother's sanity was fragile. It was a bubble that we were all engaged in blowing and we all signed a secret pact not to break it for any reason.

Second semester at Union Grade High began and your mother and I had English class together again, still with McKeever. I sat nearer to her, across the aisle, and I tried to see what she was writing in her spiral notebook. She smiled at me and moved the notebook away and kept writing. I didn't understand that she was writing her confession. I didn't understand that it had anything, let alone everything, to do with me.

When February arrived, I was preparing to run track and I was training every day and sprinting against my own time in the backyard. My mother was happy to see it and I was happy to see her, wandering around the garden, with real clothes on, confronting the sun. I was a sprinter and a broad jumper and she sat very still, watching me prepare for these events.

I was stone in love with Cat and she was a tennis player.

Half the time when I went out behind the school, I was hoping to see her hitting balls against the backboard, wearing her white shorts and a red and white striped shirt. She was exacting about tennis and if she missed a ball or simply hit one in a way she hadn't intended she would swear, then look around to see if anyone had heard her. She saw me sitting there a couple of times and we locked eyes and smiled.

You have to understand this about your mother. She was great at appearing normal. What she called "playing at normal." She had been doing it since she was a little girl. It was impossible for an average teenage boy in love to see anything beyond that mask. It was a lovely mask, a convincing mask.

I couldn't tell what she was thinking when she looked at me. I didn't know if she liked me or not. I certainly didn't know what she was planning. She was days away from handing me the letter.

But February was a good month and I went to bed in the early days feeling that life was getting back on course, that the bubble was not going to break and it was all going to be fine.

You think the letter was the thing that broke the bubble, but it wasn't.

My mother broke the bubble because someone broke it for her.

I was asleep again one night when my mother came in. This time I woke up when she opened the door so I was already awake when she came in. Even though she was dressed in normal clothes, she looked all wild and crazy. She was smoking, which she had stopped doing in the house, part of the bubble. I sat straight up.

"What's wrong?" I asked.

She put a forefinger to her lips to shush me. She looked around and said, "Today I heard something, John."

"What did you hear?"

She shook her head and looked around. She waited. No one was coming. She sat down on my bed and her cigarette was burning.

"In the garden club, I heard it," she told me.

"Okay."

I could smell on her breath that she had been drinking. My mother did that. Both my parents did that. They went out and they drank. I didn't care. It seemed to be what grown-ups did and I had no fascination with it. I assumed I'd do my fair share of it when I was their age, but I was in no hurry. Still, it wasn't lost on me that my mother smelled like that more often than my father.

Her eyes were blurry but I ignored it. I was focused on her cigarette, which was burning down. Some of the ash fell onto the floor of my bedroom.

She said, "She was having an affair. Jackie was."

I rubbed my eyes. "Yeah, yeah, the bad boyfriend."

"No, not the boyfriend. A married man. Someone well known in the community. They wouldn't say who."

"Who told you this?"

She put her cigarette out in my Coke can. "Marsha Tomkins. Her husband's a judge. She would know."

"But she didn't know who."

"I didn't say that. I said she wouldn't say."

"So what do you think, she ran off with this guy?"

She shook her head.

"He paid her to leave town?"

She trained her eyes on me and nodded. "It's the only thing that makes sense. She was probably pregnant. Probably living somewhere afraid to come home. He's keeping her. She's raising his bastard child."

"Mom, calm down," I remember saying because she was talking faster and creating this whole scenario for which she had no real proof.

But that's how much she wanted Jackie to be alive somewhere in the world, walking around, with a chance of coming back.

Instead of down a well just across town.

She said, "Then the whole town covered the mess up. Because that's what they do here. They protect each other."

"Can you find out who it was?"

"I can die trying, I'll tell you that. And I will."

"Well, I guess it's good. That she's alive."

"Yes, baby," she said. "It's good."

And then she left.

That was the last I heard of it. She never talked about it again.

And then I got the letter.

• 5 •

It was Valentine's Day. It was also the day I tried out for track. I placed first in the sprints and first in the broad jump and I was all happy about myself. I sat on the grass and caught my breath. The coach came over and told me what to do and what to expect and how to purchase my uniform. I was half listening and half watching your mother up on the tennis court. I was feeling for the first time that I might have an identity away from Charlie, something I was good at that he'd never tried, and that I had a shot at a normal adolescence.

I sat and watched the rest of the track team doing their mile and their high jump and their hurdles. I drank a Coke. The tennis team finished their maneuvers and I saw your mother sitting in the parking lot, waiting for her ride. I felt brave, so I went up there.

She was sitting on her books and looking at her watch. When I walked up to her she just looked up at me and smiled. It was like she knew I was coming.

"Hi," I said.

"Hi," she said back.

"Happy Valentine's Day," I said.

She laughed. "You, too."

"I'm John Russo."

"I know who you are," she said.

"You call me Noah," I told her.

She laughed again. She laughed a lot. But not a nervous laugh. It was relaxed and it made you relax. I can't explain it. It was just a good sound.

"Where did you hear that?" she asked.

"I listen. I'm an eavesdropper."

"Nice. Pervert," she said.

"I like that name," I told her. "Noah."

"Then I'll keep calling you that."

We remained that way for a while. Her sitting on her books and me kicking up the gravel, still in my track gear, her still in her tennis gear.

She said something like so you run track and I said yeah, I do sprints and jumps and she said the track uniforms weren't as retarded-looking as the baseball uniforms, and we laughed about that. We kind of ignored the fact that we'd been circling around each other all year. Well, we didn't ignore it. We just understood it. There was no reason to discuss it.

"You're from up North," she said. "But nobody's sure where."

"New York."

She nodded, her eyes working, as if she were trying to picture it.

She said, "I'm just biding my time here."

"Oh, really," I said. "Where are you going to?"

She said, "I want to live in California."

"Why?" I asked.

She laughed. "Why? Because the sun shines every day. And because it's three thousand miles from here."

"I get that," I said.

I looked at her. I looked at her dark wavy hair cascading down her back and her light eyes and her big smile. I looked at her legs, all tanned and muscled, and her sneakers, all beaten up from charging the court, and I didn't know what to say. I certainly couldn't tell her that I'd seen her first thing at the drugstore and that I was going to marry her.

"I don't think I'll make it, though," she said suddenly. Her voice scared me. She was staring at her sneakers and twirling her racket between her fingers.

"What do you mean?"

"To California. I don't think that's in the cards."

"Why not?"

And then she stood up, as if she heard the gravel stirring in the distance, though there was no car in sight. She unzipped her backpack and took something out of it. It was a manila envelope and it contained something that looked like a really long English essay.

But of course it was the letter.

She shoved it at me and continued to look at the ground.

"What is it?"

"It's for you. Just take it."

I didn't move. She waved it emphatically and still wouldn't look at me.

"Valentine's Day," she said. "It's appropriate."

Later she told me that she hadn't decided to give it to me until that very moment. What made her decide, I asked? She wasn't sure. The way I was looking at her. The fact that I was standing so close and having a normal conversation and she felt happy and then realized she didn't have the right to feel happy.

"And the talk of California," she admitted much later, when she realized it. "The promised land. I didn't deserve to reach it."

I held the envelope in my hand. Our eyes locked again and I wanted to say, Look, I love you, and I didn't know what to say after that. I felt I had to thank her or ask a question.

Her father's green Ford LTD pulled up and I said, "What is it?"

"Just read it. I've explained everything. But don't talk to me."

"Don't talk to you when?"

"Ever. I have to go."

The green Ford LTD pulled up right in front of us and her

father was at the wheel and I watched her get into the car and then the car drove away. I hardly even noticed him. Because I didn't understand it yet, I didn't know what I was looking for.

I read the whole letter that night. I didn't entirely get it, so I put it under my mattress and went to sleep. I woke up in the middle of the night and read it again.

I knew it was all true.

How do you know the truth, even when it sounds bizarre? It's a matter of discernment. That's what religious people call it. It's what lawyers call it, too. You have to be able to know when someone is lying to you.

The best I can tell you is this: The truth always settles on you very quietly, and it sits in a pocket inside you and doesn't displace anything and it just feels right but not always logical. Logic is something else. The truth is quiet and simple but not painless.

The truth just is.

And this just was.

I wish I could tell you I was shocked or I saw my life flash before my eyes or I felt some grand emotion or had an epiphany. Maybe that's all true. I just don't remember it. I remember reading the letter once, reading it again, and knowing it was true. I guess I thought about what it would do to my mother, but I probably thought more about what it would do to my chances with Cat.

I couldn't get a clear picture of that. After all, the last thing she had said to me was not to talk to her again. I knew that wasn't possible so I didn't even entertain the idea. I knew I was going to find her as quickly as I could, and probably I was concocting some kind of grand scheme or speech. I was plotting a way for us to run off together. Maybe I fantasized about buying bus tickets. I honestly can't remember.

What I can remember was feeling like the other shoe had dropped. All the theories were evaporating into the ether and the thing I had always known to be true was coming into focus. Only I had never pictured Jackie's murderer as someone I knew. I had never pictured him driving a green Ford LTD or being the father of the girl I loved.

I had never pictured her witnessing it. I didn't know that you could see such a thing and get up in the morning and go about your business. And eventually become a beautiful high school girl who doesn't wear makeup and whose laugh could set people at ease. I didn't see a normal attractive girl coming out of that scenario and making the tennis team. It's just not the way we are trained to see the children of monsters emerging.

I don't know why, though. We've seen enough photos of the Nazi children in their crisp school uniforms holding pets and smiling at the camera. I must have known it was possible. It's just a paradox, I suppose. The impossible task of holding two opposing thoughts in your head at once. We think it can't be done, yet we do it all the time. The way children of crazy alcoholic mothers think it's all going to be fine tomorrow. The way an entire nation can nuke another country across the Pacific and still believe in patriotism and humanity. The way a self-made businessman can kill a little girl and think it is all in the best interest of his family.

We live with opposing thoughts. As if it is what we were born to do.

I suppose you do it even better when you're young.

And the reason for that is, you think that your youth negates your behavior and your knowledge because it is only age that is going to qualify your experience. You think it's only what you do once you're an adult that matters. And what you're going to do as an adult is be perfect.

Perfection looms. Even though no one else has achieved it.

No one else has ever been you.

And I was so sure of all this flawed logic that I didn't even toss and turn or worry about what it would do to my existence as I knew it or to my history as I would perceive it later. Certainly not how it would sound to my daughter a couple of decades later.

I just knew the truth was under my pillow and I went to sleep.

• 6 •

"What are we going to do?"

This was your mother.

She was sitting under a tree in the woods behind the high school. It's where people went to smoke cigarettes and dope and drink beer during lunch. We weren't doing any of that. We were yards away from that group and we felt their eyes on us occasionally, but because we weren't snitches and we didn't want their stash, we were invisible to them.

She was wearing a faded bandanna over her long hair and a Danskin leotard and sailor jeans and gold hoops in her ears. A gold cross fell right between her breasts and I tried not to look at that. Oh, sorry, honey, I forgot. You don't want to hear about your mother's breasts. What I'm trying to say is that I was so in love with her. And she wasn't having any of it. It wasn't on her mind. Because your mom was a warrior and a crusader. She was a brave person. I was a teenage boy in love.

And because I was a teenage boy in love, I had chased her down the halls, stood outside her classes, passed her notes in English, until she finally relented and agreed to see me during lunch. I had approached the day with nothing but the determination to wear her down. I wasn't going to accept her plan of never speaking to me again. It seemed dramatic and girly and it just wasn't going to stand.

Not that your mother had no resolve. She had plenty of it. But she hadn't met mine yet. She had simply reawakened it.

"What do you mean?" I asked.

"How are we going to fix it?" she said, a little impatient with me. "I mean, your idea was to fix it. That was your pitch. That was how you got me to talk to you again."

"Right," I said, "because I have a plan."

"Yeah, so? Let's hear your plan."

I was momentarily silent.

Then she said, as if I needed reminding, "My father killed your cousin."

"Yeah, I know."

"I saw him do it."

"You didn't do anything wrong."

"How can you say that? I was there. I helped."

"You were a little girl."

"I kept his secret. I've been keeping it. I'm not a little girl now."

"But you did say something. You told me. You must have told me for a reason."

"I'm culpable," she said, and her eyes were full of tears.

I was trying to remember what culpable was.

Don't laugh, Lynnie. Don't think I was an idiot, either, or someone without a soul. It's just that I had always known Jackie was dead and I had always known someone had killed her and I didn't know Cat's father at all but I knew her. It didn't surprise me that he was a criminal because I was from New York, where everybody knew all powerful men were most likely connected and there was corruption everywhere and people tried to work around it. Nobody in Manhattan thought that crime was confined to the gutters. Only a certain kind of crime. The high-level stuff happened in the boardrooms and the churches and the schools.

That kind of crime was protected. It never came out into the open unless someone was brave enough to take a stand. That's what she was trying to do. That was what I was trying to do. And we were both kids.

None of this meant that Cat was a criminal. It meant she was an innocent. More than that, she was an avenger. That was a word I knew from comic books, but I knew it and I took it seriously.

"Does your father know?" I asked her.

She smirked. "Does he know he killed her?"

"Does he know you remember? And that you're talking about it?"

"Are you crazy? He would kill me. I'm risking my life here."

Maybe that was when it hit me. Maybe that was when I

stopped thinking of kissing her and started thinking of saving her. She was staring at me with those big green eyes and I was helpless.

I put my arm around her and pulled her close and she let me. I said, "Okay, we'll tell them."

"Who? The police? My dad's golf buddies?" she said.

So I told her, "Not the cops. My parents."

She stared at me. She asked the right question:

"What are they gonna do?"

I didn't know. I shook my head again. I was trying to think, trying to make my brain work as fast as hers, willing myself to be as smart. I was as smart, almost, but my brain had been asleep for a long time. It had been sleeping against the reality of my mother's condition and against the reality of Charlie being gone and sometimes the plain old mundane reality of my hormones. Sorry, Lynne. You have to hear about hormones. It's a story about teenagers.

So I woke myself up from all those forms of sleep, and sitting there on the ground under a tree next to your mother in 1975 with the oil shortage and the price gouging and the aftermath of Watergate and all the good music drifting out of passing cars and the stoners staring at us and final exams looming, I resolved to be a man and face what was coming to me. To us.

And I told her something that I've believed since that day:

"When you have to do the right thing you don't worry about what happens next. You just do it. And you trust that doing the right thing will get you through somehow. And you don't worry about dying because living with it is worse."

It was a good speech and a good principle, but your mom, who was no idiot, made a good point, too:

"Easy for you to say."

So we decided to tell my parents.

That was the obvious move, but it took courage and resolve and a certain amount of forethought. We met for a few days after our team practices and formulated the plan. We wrote stuff down. We practiced our parts, we role-played, we even prayed. And during that time we also fell in love. Well, I was already in love. Your mother started to come around during those few days. And it wasn't just because I was her rescuer, either. Though that had to have had a certain appeal. It was more because for the first time she was able to trust someone and she was starting to see a way out and a life and happiness and all the things she had given up on when she was a little girl standing in the woods two weeks before Christmas.

In my head, I could already see us married and having children. Down the road, you know. With this story backing up our union, giving it a kind of weight and a platform that no one could undermine. I grew up very fast in those few days. I was only fifteen, about to turn sixteen, and in some ways I felt exactly like that boy, a guy running track and trying to get good grades and get into college and wanting to take this cute girl to the movies. But I also knew that I was a man who had already lived through some powerful difficulties and who was about to face the challenge of a lifetime.

In my head, the challenge was how to keep my parents from blaming Cat.

I didn't think they would. I thought they would be rational and would picture her, as I had no trouble doing, as a little girl running through the woods, away from her own father. She was trying to survive. She hadn't told because of that survival instinct. And now she was telling, even though it was taking every bit of fortitude she had. Even though it meant her father would go to jail and her whole life would be disrupted. I didn't say destroyed, even to myself, because I knew she was thinking it and sometimes I let myself think it but then I remembered that my parents, let alone any kind of merciful God, would never let an innocent girl be punished.

This I told her while we sat in the parking lot, waiting for her father's green Ford LTD to arrive. I always walked away before the car drove up, at her request. She didn't want him to see me. She didn't want him to suspect anything. She wanted to keep me out of it until she couldn't anymore.

It made my blood run cold to see her getting into that car. I'd watch from a distance, near the track field, so far away that I couldn't see her features and I couldn't see him at all. But I knew there was evil in that car, and the girl I loved was getting in and riding shotgun.

Are you okay? You look pale. We can stop now. I can tell you later.

It's very late.

Well, have some water and I'll keep going.

• 7 •

We sat in the living room of the horrible pseudo-Colonial house in Union Grade, Virginia. My mother, who had dressed up as if she were going to a PTA meeting, and my father, who had come home early from his dental practice because, as it had been sold to him by Mother, "John is bringing a girl home for dinner."

We had no intention of eating dinner, but that was what my mother had in mind, so she had made a meat loaf, which was in the oven, and some canapés, which were spread in a fancy way in front of us, as if we were the bridge club. Dad mixed himself a drink and Mother declined one, which was unusual for her. She was showing off for Cat. After all, she knew Cat's mom. She told her so. Such a nice lady. Made such an effort to be kind when we moved here. Our Charlie is your sister's age. He's at Chapel Hill. Architecture. Football. He has a girlfriend. We haven't met her. We think she's Asian but he won't say.

I barely heard any of this. Neither did Cat. She was pulling on the sleeves of her black sweater and staring at the carpet and forcing a smile.

My mother was firmly lodged in the bubble. She was fully functional and willing to believe that her life could be normal and she could be in the position of simply entertaining my girl-friend, the daughter of a local prominent citizen. These kinds of things made her happy.

My father was a little more connected to the mood. He saw

the way I was sitting forward in my seat and chewing my nails and looking only at Cat.

He said, "How do you kids know each other?"

"We have English together," I said. "But that's not why we're here."

"Darling, we know why you're here," Mother said. "You want us to meet your friend, and we're happy to do that. We're happy to meet you, Catherine."

She looked up and smiled and didn't say call me Cat, because she didn't care.

"No, I mean, there's something else."

"Yes, we know. You're dating. We picked up on that a long time ago." Mother laughed. She liked to be the intuitive, sophisticated one. Ahead of the game. It was a way to prove her sanity, which, I saw to my frustration, was something she could trot out when she felt like it, as if it were the good china.

"Well, dating," my father said also with a mild laugh. "As much as anyone can date without a car."

I didn't have a car, either, Lynne. You'll find this ironic.

I had been begging them for Charlie's old car, which still lived at home because he had nowhere to park it at college, but they were refusing, saying it still officially belonged to Charlie, and if I wanted my own car I could work and buy one the way he had. I was a few months away from getting my license, so it was a future issue.

"I know, they don't call it dating. They call it going together," Mother said, showing off more of her urbane wit. Trying to fit in. "One wants to ask, going where? Where are you going? As Daddy says, you don't even have a car. But I know just what you mean. We called it going steady. I suppose that sounds archaic to you."

"Mother," I said, "it's a little more serious than that."

The room and all its nervous activity came to a halt. I saw the canapés—crab and mushrooms and olives on thin bread—sweating in the stale air of the living room, and I thought of my mother planning and cutting off the crusts and picturing an evening right out of Tennessee Williams or a Jerome Kern song. My mother was a romantic, which probably the thing that made her so crazy, always seeing things in a dramatic light, always letting them grow larger than life, like a sponge in water.

When I said that, Cat looked at me and her face stalled, because now she knew it was all going to happen. I wasn't going to back out. The truth was going to come out and her whole life was about to change. Her eyes landed hard on me and I just nodded at her to let her know I was in charge when, in reality, I had no idea what I was going to say, just that I was going to say it.

My parents went to an entirely different place altogether. I should have seen it coming. But I was too stupid. Stupid in love, stupid in purpose and planning, stupid in all the ways I was going to save the girl I loved.

My mother put her palm to her chest and said, "Oh, my God."

My father stood and swirled the Scotch around the ice in his glass.

He said, "Now hold on, everybody. This is just a problem. Problems have solutions. Let's not get ahead of ourselves."

"Right," I said, still stupid. "That's what I keep telling Cat. It's just a problem."

My mother had turned pale. She got up and went to the bar and poured herself a drink. My father was staring daggers at me. Cat was staring at me that way, too, because she knew and she was not being stupid and she was feeling completely let down by my inability to grasp the situation.

Mother turned once her vodka glass was full and she said, "How far along?"

"What?" I asked.

Cat closed her eyes and looked away from me. She shook her head slowly.

"How far along," my mother said, enunciating her words in an angry and deliberate manner, as she once used to say "Go to your room."

"Far along what?" I asked.

Cat's head was bowed so far forward that her dark hair was covering her face. I felt lost.

"These things can be handled," my father was saying.

"What things?"

My mother stood up straight and pointed her vodka glass at Cat and said, "She's pregnant. For God's sake, just say it."

"Ella," my father said quietly.

Cat just stared at the carpet. I saw her shoulders shaking. I didn't know if she was laughing or crying. I reached out to touch her and she swatted my hand away.

"Wait," I said. "Wait."

Cat stood and said, "I should go home now."

"No, Cat, sit down," I told her.

She did.

My parents were staring at me. I was embarrassed and proud all at once. Embarrassed—that's obvious. Proud that my parents thought I was mature and brave and frankly skilled enough to accomplish something like that at fifteen. I was a virgin—yes, men can be virgins, too. And so was your mother. And we had never gotten anywhere close to sex. I still felt lucky that she let me touch her hand. Which, in that moment, she wouldn't let me do.

"No," I said. "No, Cat's not pregnant."

I had a strange moment where I wanted to ask her if she was in fact pregnant, pregnant with someone else's baby, feeling that my crazy mother with all her weird intuition had picked up on something I had missed. But I knew she wasn't pregnant and I took a breath and reconnected with reality and reminded myself what we were all doing there.

"No," I said again. "Cat and I aren't . . . we aren't like that. Nobody's pregnant."

My father let out a breath but my mother was standing hard and straight, staring at me. She took a long drink from her vodka glass and said, "Well, if that's the case, what can be wrong? What can be so serious?"

I thought about what to say. I was choosing my words. But before I could even put a sentence together, I heard Cat talking.

Your mother always had the gift of truth. You saw it in her; you experienced it. She never lied to you. When you were tiny and you asked her if ghosts were real, she simply said, "I don't know, honey, but I know they can't hurt you." When you asked if she was going to die, she'd say, "Well, I can die, but I don't think I'm going to." When you asked if dead people went to heaven, she'd say, "Oh, I hope so." I'm not telling you anything you don't already know about her. Your mother was infected and besieged and haunted by the truth. She didn't know how to say anything else.

Once I asked her why she didn't soft sell the world to you, when you were just a tiny child. I asked, "Why can't you let her make believe while she's little?" She said, "I'm afraid she'll make believe all her life."

As she had been forced to do. Until she couldn't anymore.

This is what she said:

"Mrs. Russo, I knew your niece, Jackie. She was my babysitter when I was little. She was only a little older than my sister but my parents called on her to look out for us when they went out at night. She came by in the afternoons to play with us so my mother could get some work done or take a nap. We loved her. I loved her. She was my favorite babysitter."

I saw my mother's posture softening.

Cat went on.

She said, "Her father worked in my father's carpet plant as a machinist. They were poor and it was made clear to us that we couldn't really socialize with Jackie or her sisters. But I loved her anyway. I didn't understand any of that. Jackie had the wild boyfriend who came to see her on the motorcycle, but he was never mean to her or to us. She didn't run away with him."

My mother was paralyzed by Cat's voice but she somehow found the energy to say, "What makes you say that? Everyone thinks she ran away with that boy. My sister thinks it to this day."

"No," Cat said.

"Well, yes, there is the rumor that she was involved with

someone in town. And he paid her to disappear," my mother said, ready to shift to another reality.

"No," Cat said.

"What do you mean, 'no'?" my mother demanded. "You can't possibly know for sure."

"No," Cat said. "She was murdered."

"That's only a theory," Mother said.

"No, it's not a theory, it's a fact."

My mother let out a little cry and my father moved to her side.

"I think this is enough," he said. "I think we've heard enough for one night."

"Let her finish," I said.

Cat kept talking.

She said, "I know she was murdered because I saw it."

She went on to say how she saw it. She described it much as she had done with me. My mother completely checked out somewhere in there. My father helped lower her to a chair but he remained alert, standing and listening intently. The only thing I said while all this was going on was that Cat had written me a letter about it and I still owned it and my father wanted to know where it was and I didn't answer.

Cat finished up her story by saying, "So I really needed to tell someone that. I told Noah, and now I have to tell you."

My father said, "Who's Noah?"

I said, "It's her nickname for me. Never mind."

I could see him using this against her in his head.

My mother was now finished with her water glass of vodka and her eyes were distant and drooping. My father put his hand on her shoulder.

He said, "You kids have too much time on your hands. Obviously, you need to find a hobby."

Cat looked at me.

I looked at my parents.

My mother was thinking about nodding off and my father was staring hot embers into me and I didn't know what to do.

I said, "Dad, I believe her. I think it's the truth. I mean, the whole reason we moved here was to find out."

"No," he said. "We moved here to give your mother some peace. Is this your idea of giving her peace?"

My mother said, "Baby Jackie was my little girl. The girl I never had."

Cat just stared at her.

There was another lull and my father grew angry and slammed his glass down and said, "Goddamn you kids. What will you think of next? Do you really want to kill us? Is that your whole plan?"

Cat stood up again and said, "I have to leave."

"No," I said.

"I told you they wouldn't believe us."

My mother stood and said, "I have to go to bed."

She stumbled off in the direction of the stairs.

My father walked right up to me and said, "I need to talk to you alone. In the kitchen."

I told Cat not to leave. I had no idea if she would or wouldn't.

My father and I went to the kitchen and he turned off the oven where the meat loaf was sizzling and probably burning. I sat down at the table and he paced and I waited. He turned on me finally.

He said, "Do you know who her father is?"

"Yeah, sure. He runs the carpet factory and he's on the town council and he's a deacon in the church. So what? You think criminals are all disheveled and homeless?"

My father said, "He's an important man in this town."

"He sets fires."

"He what?"

"He's an arsonist. Ask around. He does it in his free time."

"I suppose this is something she told you."

"One of the things. But other people must know it."

"John, he's practically the mayor."

"So?"

My father shook his head and drained the last of his Scotch. He put his empty glass in the sink.

"Let's say this is true. Let's say your new girlfriend's father is an arsonist and a murderer. While also being a prominent citizen. Who do you think is going to believe us here? We're not from this town. We're interlopers. Do you really think I'm going to start a crusade against him?"

"Dad, I don't know, but Mom has spent most of the last few years wanting to know who killed Jackie, and Cat is telling you."

"It's a lie," he said.

"It's not a lie."

"She's trying to impress you."

"Why would she use that to impress me? She avoided talking to me for months when we first moved here because she was so afraid of telling me. It took a real act of courage to tell me. She's putting her life on the line here."

My father rubbed his face with his hands as if trying to wake himself up from a bad dream. Then he stared at me.

"This cannot be true. Do you understand? Even if it's true, it can't be true. Do you understand?"

"No."

"She's manipulating you. I've spent the last half hour looking at her. My God, John, you can do better. Would you really throw your life away for this girl?"

I stared at him. I didn't understand the question. But I already knew the answer.

"Yes, I would," I said.

He didn't like that. He ignored it.

"This is the last we're going to say of the matter. Now get her out of here. I have to go take care of your mother."

He left me alone.

I sat in the kitchen for what seemed like a long time. I heard the pops and clicks of the oven cooling down. I heard my father walking around upstairs. I heard their mumbled voices in the bedroom. I finally found the muscles in my legs and I walked back into the living room. Cat was sitting there, staring at a wall, chewing on her shirtsleeve.

She looked at me and gave me a sad smile and she stood.

"They'll come around," I promised without any evidence.

We stood face to face.

She kissed me on the cheek and walked out and didn't close the door behind her.

So much for my plan.

• 8 •

High school went on the way it always had except that Cat wouldn't look at me.

Our track team made it to the semifinals and the tennis team made it that far, too, so as late as May, we were all meeting in the parking lot, waiting for our rides. I knew all the reasons Cat couldn't look at me and I didn't know what to do. Sometimes I hovered near her while she sat on her books and wrote in a notebook. I wondered if she was writing me another letter. But a couple of times when I got close enough to look over her shoulder, I saw that she was just doing math equations. I felt as if the whole business between us had been a strange dream.

It was the beginning of June, when school was so close to being over we all felt cranky and excited and ready to say anything that I approached her. She didn't look at me as I talked. She was twirling her racket in her hands and staring at the motion.

Our conversation went like this:

"Hi, Cat. Did you win today?"

"Yeah, I took my match. Straight sets."

"Congratulations. Did the team win?"

"Tie."

"Bummer."

The next day I asked her if she was ready for exams. She said she was worried about geometry. I said I was worried about English.

The next day I asked if she had cut her hair. It looked different. She said she had trimmed the ends, that was all.

And it went that way for a while, these formal conversations, her never looking at me, and me thrashing around for questions.

But this one day, when I felt courageous, about twelve days from school letting out, I sat down next to her and said, "Cat, we have to talk."

"We have been talking."

"No, not really."

She stared at the ground and shook her head.

"Don't," she said.

"I'm not giving up."

"You should."

"Look, I believe you. The fact that my parents couldn't believe you doesn't mean it's over."

"It's over, John."

"Only if you say so."

Finally she looked at me. "I'm saying so."

"You're making a mistake."

She didn't say anything. She picked up a strand of hair and started inspecting the ends. I wanted to grab her.

"How can you do this?" I nearly yelled at her. She looked up at me calmly.

"Do what?"

"Act like it's all okay . . . it's all normal."

"For me it is normal."

"Not for me."

"You'll have to learn to live with it."

"I get it that you've worked out a whole system. But I'm not there yet. This is driving me crazy."

"Get used to it."

"I can't."

"Play along."

"I won't live like that."

Now I was yelling and now she was looking at me, and so were some kids standing nearby, but I ignored them. There were tears in her eyes. I had gotten a reaction. I had broken through the mask.

She said, "Your family . . . Jackie's family . . . they're the only reason I told in the first place. For her. To make it okay for her. Because I knew her and I wanted to help and I . . ."

She stopped talking and put her face in her hands.

I hated to see her cry. I didn't know what to do. I knew enough not to touch her, though.

"I think we should go to the cops."

She laughed. She said, "My dad is the cops."

"He is?"

"The town council oversees the cops. They all know him. They play golf. They go to our church. Don't make me explain how this all works."

"I know how it works. But there has to be one honest guy in Union Grade."

She actually smiled at me, brushing away tears. "I think it might be you."

I was so happy to see her smile I could barely form a thought. But I knew I had to keep her on track.

Cat said, "Like those ridiculous five minutes when your

parents thought I was pregnant. Remember what your dad said? These things can be handled."

"Yeah, I remember. But . . ."

"That's how everybody sees everything in this town. It can be handled. My father is a first-class handler. And he's not even in the inner sanctum. He's just acquainted with it. It goes deep. That's all I'm saying. And I don't even know why I'm saying this much."

She stood up then and I had to stop her. It felt like my last chance because I knew it would get harder and harder to talk to her about this or anything.

"Just go with me. I'll do the talking. I'm an outsider so they'll have to listen to me."

"You're not an outsider. Your dad's rich."

"We're from up North."

"He's a doctor. You're in."

"All we can do is try, Cat. If we tell the cops and nothing happens, then we can know that nothing was supposed to happen."

"Nothing was supposed to happen? Body down the well and moving on?"

I stood and touched her arm and she let me. I said, "Her parents are gone. They moved away. They might have adjusted to a new life somewhere. My mother has lost it and she just wants to believe Jackie's alive somewhere. If nothing happens it might mean that the damage is done and everybody's better off. I don't think so and neither do you. We have to try. We don't have anything to lose."

"If my father finds out, I have something to lose."

"What's he gonna do, ground you?"

152

"Kill me, John. Just like he promised a long time ago."

"It was a threat. To a child."

She thought about it. I could see her remembering. And then updating, seeing herself as she was now, almost an adult.

I said, "If we don't try, it's going to follow us for the rest of our lives. I believe that."

She looked at me just as her father's car drove up.

"Tomorrow afternoon. We'll meet here," I said.

"I have a game," she answered.

"I do, too."

She nodded. The games didn't matter.

And my last act of defiance, or reassurance, was to kiss her on the cheek right there in front of God and her father, and her mouth dropped open and I knew I would take care of her forever if she'd let me.

· 9 ·

There was only one police station for the entire town of Union Grade, Virginia, and we sat in the waiting chairs for a long time. Finally a uniformed police officer came out to greet us. We stood up and shook his hand. His name was Billy Campbell. He was all of twenty-eight. He wanted us to call him Officer Campbell. And he wanted us to know he was very busy and asked if it would take long. I said it might. He stared at me, sizing me up, because the real question was whether or not it was serious and my eyes told him it was.

Then he looked at Cat and said, "How're your folks doing, Cat? I saw your dad on the golf course Saturday."

153

"They're fine."

"Haven't seen you on the course in a while."

"I have tennis."

"I guess that takes up time. You on the tennis team, too? Sorry, I forgot your name."

"I never said it," I told him. We were following him to his desk. Cops were watching us and I could feel Cat shrinking into her clothes.

"John Russo," I told him, "and I run track."

"Russo, that's Italian?"

"American. By way of Italy, I guess."

"Your dad's the dentist."

"Yep."

We got to Officer Campbell's desk and it was only a few feet away from a few other officers' desks, and I saw Cat looking around. Then she looked at me and her eyes were pleading. I could see her losing her nerve.

I said, "Officer Campbell, we might need some privacy for this."

"Privacy?" he laughed. "This is Union Grade. We don't have any privacy."

Cat shook her head at me.

I said, "Isn't there another room?"

He looked at me and said, "There's the interrogation room, but that's for interrogations."

"You can ask us questions, then."

I was trying to be funny so he'd like us. He looked at his watch and finally said all right and he shouted to the other cops, "Boys, I got the interrogation room for the next five or so. Try not to arrest anybody."

They laughed.

The interrogation room was just a room with a table and some folding chairs and a window, but not even a two-way mirror like they had on TV even back then. Cat and I sat down and I started talking while Officer Campbell was still pouring himself some coffee.

I told him the whole story without stopping and Cat chewed on her sweater sleeve and Officer Campbell looked from me to her and forgot to drink his coffee.

When I was finished he just pushed the cup aside and put his hands in prayer position and touched his bottom lip and stared just above my head. It seemed to take forever. I was holding Cat's hand under the table and it was cold and dry.

Finally, Officer Campbell looked at her but spoke to me.

"That's quite a story, Mr. Russo."

"It's her story. But she wanted me to tell it."

"The question is whether or not it's true. Cat?"

"Why would I make it up?" she said.

"I don't know. Your dad grounded you for something. Or he won't let you go out with Mr. Russo. Or he won't buy you a new car."

"I love my father," she said.

"Really. You love him. According to this, then, you love a murdering maniac."

"He's not a maniac. He's a criminal. And he's my father."

"You love him so much you want him to get arrested and go to prison?"

"I want to do the right thing."

"I see."

"Because of her."

"Who's that?"

She looked at him as if he were crazy or evil or stupid.

"Jackie," she said in a whisper.

He nodded.

Cat stood and said, "Never mind, I knew he wouldn't believe us."

"I didn't say that. Sit down, Cat."

She sat down.

"I've known your dad since I was little; my father and him are friends, so you can imagine how hard it is to hear."

"Not as hard as it was to see."

He sat back in his chair.

"I only brought up these other possibilities because I have to. I can't just take a teenager's word for something. Hell, everybody in town would get arrested."

"You don't have to take my word. Go look down the well."

"Go look down the well. You know how many abandoned wells there are in those woods? You know what it takes to look down one? Cameras won't reach that far. We'd have to send a man. With the unstable sides and all, I'd be risking someone's life. Look down a well, she says."

Cat bowed her head, as if she were ashamed. I wanted to hit him.

She didn't cry, though. Cat was too proud for that.

"Here's what I'm going to do," Officer Campbell said. "I'm going to get a notepad and pen and you're going to write all this down and sign it. After that I'll give it to my supervisor and he'll make a decision about how to proceed. Does that sound okay?"

She nodded.

"Do you want something to drink while I'm at it? Coke? Water?"

She shook her head. He didn't ask me if I wanted anything.

He excused himself and left the room. Cat and I didn't look at each other or say anything. I just held her hand and she let me. It didn't take him long to come back with the pen and paper and he brought her a Coke anyway. Then he said, "I'm going to give you some privacy while you're doing this. Just write it down like you told me. In detail. Much as you can remember. Then come find me out in the bull pen. Okay?"

She nodded.

"Mr. Russo, it'd be better if you waited outside. We got magazines out there."

I looked at Cat and she nodded that it was okay, so I went with him.

I was looking at a back issue of *Field & Stream,* trying to stay interested because I didn't care about fields or streams, when I heard a commotion at the front of the station and I looked up to see Cat's father.

I'd never really seen him but I knew it was him.

She looked like him. That was a scary moment. She had his eyes. He wasn't smiling, but if he had been, it would have been her smile, too.

He was wearing a suit and he was talking in a loud voice to the desk officer, and Officer Campbell was hurrying over to him. He gestured for him to keep his voice down. It all came together in that moment and I got up and hurried to the room where Cat was and Officer Campbell saw me and yelled for me to stop right there. I thought I could get shot but I didn't care.

I flung the door open and said to Cat, "He's here. Let's go."

She knew who I meant and her face went pale and she said, "Go where?"

"Out the window."

"And then where?"

"We'll figure that out later. Stop arguing."

She stood up very slowly and said, "John, there's nowhere to go."

And I said, "Cat, I'll take care of you, trust me."

She gave me this really sad smile with her lips pressed together and she still wasn't crying and the door burst open and there was her father and it was all over.

• 10 •

"Over? What do you mean over?"

My pulse was thumping like I was in the break zone of a wave. I was caught up in the story. I was seeing my mother, just the way I remembered her, all happy and optimistic and singing, getting into a car with a criminal, a killer no less, and I actually thought she might die. I mean, long before she actually did die, long before she married my father and had me.

All of it was such a shock, it wouldn't have surprised me to hear that the woman I knew was not my actual mother. My father wasn't my father. I was adopted. Left on the doorstep. He was in the CIA. We were actually aliens. Where did it end?

"What do you mean over?" I asked again.

"The fight," he said. "That was over."

"How could you have kept this from me? I didn't get a chance to know my mother as she really was. I loved some imposter."

"That's not true."

"She was just acting the whole time."

"Of course not. It was a defense."

"Is that lawyer talk for phony?"

"There were things she chose to keep to herself. She had that right. You were too young to understand. Loving her family, that was not an act."

"I don't know what to believe. You lied to me."

"I didn't."

"By not telling me, you were lying."

He said, "Lynnie, try to think it through. I know it's a lot but you're a smart kid. Think it through."

I wanted to kick his chair out from under him. I loved him and all, but what was this think-it-through business? It was at times like this that I missed having a woman in the house the most. My father, like all men according to our group discussions at Hillsboro, was about thinking, not feeling, and he thought all things could be solved by logic. He was not going to be able to logic his way out of this one, though. This was going to require some down-and-dirty emotions.

"Okay, I'm thinking. I've got nothing."

"You were in the third grade when she died. You could barely add."

"I was multiplying in the second grade."

"You were a child. You slept with a night-light."

"I did not."

He raised his chin at me.

Maybe I did.

"You could have found some way to tell me," I argued. "Or she could have. For God's sake, she told me about sex when I was four."

"Because you asked."

"I wasn't ready to know. It completely freaked me out. I think that's when I started sleeping with a night-light. She was always doing that to me, Dad. Remember when I loved the Beatles in preschool? I asked her where John Lennon was now and she told me. In detail. I remember going to school and explaining it to my classmates. Their mothers called her and yelled. Don't you remember that?"

He laughed, looking off. He remembered it but not as something traumatic or even disturbing. For him it was just a nice memory, an example of who she was and what he loved about her.

"She was so completely truthful about everything. That was what you always told me. And the whole time, she had this big secret she was keeping from her own kid."

"We made a judgment call, Lynnie. We decided not to let you know until you were a teenager. Now, if she had lived, we might have changed our minds. But she didn't live. And I had to abide by our original agreement. I'm sorry if you think I made a bad decision. It wasn't the first, it won't be the last. But I'm doing the best I can."

I hated the best-I-can speech. He gave it to me a lot. And when it happened I felt too guilty to listen. Because underneath it I felt the message was: I never bargained on raising you alone. I miss my wife. I was in it for her. I know he didn't really feel that way all the time. I'd also had to endure on numerous occasions the you're-all-I-have speech, and that one made me feel resentful. It made me feel he loved me too much and I was responsible for his happiness, and I couldn't live up to it.

I said, "Do you have any idea what it feels like to find out that your parents aren't who you thought they were?"

"Of course," he said. "Every teenager finds that out. Nobody is who you think they are when you're young. You have a childish view of them. Your own parents are the first victims of your burgeoning ability to see things as they are. The scales fall off your eyes by degrees. And the first thing in front of you are the people who raised you and they can never bear up to your scrutiny."

He was raising his voice now and had gotten a little fancy on me.

Probably because I wasn't having the reaction he'd expected. I knew he wanted me to be all sentimental and weepy over my mother now. He was imagining me throwing my arms around him and saying, "Thank you for not getting me a car, it's so much better to have criminals in the family."

I was feeling a lot of things but that wasn't one of them.

"What's the point of it all, then?" I asked, my throat tightening, but I was still raging against the tears. "I'm supposed to realize you guys had a hard time in life? And that's supposed to make me want to have a hard time in life, too? Well, guess what, Dad, I'm having it. I've been having it since the bad car wreck and this isn't helping."

I threw the manuscript across the room in an ugly way that made me feel at once like a brat and also a hell of a lot better.

He stared at the scattered papers. I could tell he wanted to start picking them up. I could tell he also wanted to hit me. I knew because I wanted to hit him, too. I wanted us to get into a boxing match now.

"You don't know how to do this," I screamed at him. "You don't know the first thing about it."

"About what?"

"This," I said, making a wild gesture. "Everything. Raising me. The way she would have."

"No, of course not. I'm not her."

"Doing your best? You aren't even trying!"

"Trying what? My God, Lynnie . . ."

"You're not trying anything. You just work and come home and read and think about her. Like she's still here. Like she's walking around somewhere. You don't even date. You don't even think about it. And now this, showing me this, thinking it's going to change things somehow. Did you think giving me the letter was going to make something happen? It was going to conjure her up? Make her come back to life? Or did you think it would make her some kind of saint? Somebody would build a statue to her?"

He looked into his lap. He said, "I thought it would help you understand her."

"No, Dad, it's the other thing. It makes me wonder if I knew her at all."

"Are you blaming her?" he asked.

"No."

"Because if you are, I don't know you at all."

"You're right about that."

He stood and started picking up the pages, one by one,

whipping them from the floor to his chest, like plucking oysters, each one of which contained a pearl.

"It was not her fault. She did the right thing. She wasn't a saint but she was good. And she was the bravest person I ever knew."

"And I'll never be her."

He straightened up and held the papers close to him and fixed his gaze on me.

"You are part of her."

"I'll never be as good."

"That," he said, "is a choice."

He took the papers and walked out of the room and left me alone, just like that, with the bird bracelet and the candles. And all the history and guilt and anger and sadness bouncing off the walls and me feeling like I was coming apart, dissolving like paper in water, and I grabbed my head and pulled on my hair and cried without making noise.

SIXTEEN
and Officially Three Days

• 1 •

So. Jamba Juice. A date with a boy from the cemetery. It was kind of hard to get excited about that after the night I had had.

But it was the only thing I could think about that had a chance of keeping me awake during science and Latin and oh, my God, history, with Ms. Kintner dressed like a corporate Barbie and talking about how horrible we were to the Native Americans. We all felt bad about it but she actually cried, and I wanted to say, Look, I've got genocide right in my own family, in my DNA, so buck up. I didn't say it.

It was bad enough to think it.

See, being a privileged liberal private-school girl, all those stories about atrocities were just stories to me. They were my politics. My father's politics. But for the first time that day, watching Ms. Kintner cry all over her Calvin Klein suit (which I'm sure she got at Ross Dress for Less), it was suddenly real for me and I felt the way-too-familiar lump forming in my throat. I knew I couldn't actually cry, because the girls would see it and ridicule me—they were all doodling in their notebooks and thinking about lunch. They wouldn't have understood and they couldn't feel the way that I felt. Because I was picturing all those Indian people, mothers and daughters and fathers and sons, dying in the middle of their ordinary days, just because someone wanted to live on their land. And I was picturing a red-haired girl going down a well because she knew too much and was going to mess up a perfect life, which was nothing but a lie to begin with. And I was picturing my mother, not much older than me, getting on a bus and riding into a mystery, which became her freedom and her life and eventually me.

It was too much.

And I didn't want to give my father the satisfaction of knowing I was thinking that way.

The letter had changed me. That's what he was hoping for. He was hoping it would make me see my mother as a hero, as an even greater person than I imagined or remembered. But I wasn't there yet. I was just trying to process it, to get to know her all over again.

What he hadn't counted on was that it changed how I saw him. I saw him as even sadder and more stuck in the past. And I saw that what he expected of me was completely impossible.

So I stared out the window and thought about Mick.

I couldn't remember what he looked like.

I couldn't remember if I liked him or had any interest in seeing him again.

But I did remember that he was an artist and I liked that about him even though his fingers were stained from charcoal pencils, which was either gross or cool, I couldn't decide.

And I knew that I needed to do something that afternoon to distract myself. I couldn't stand the thought of sitting in my room with that letter somewhere in the house and a father who didn't get me, and all those thoughts bouncing through my brain and the music on the iPod only making it worse, making it more dramatic and heartbreaking. I was too wound up to surf and probably the only thing I had the stamina for was drinking a fruit smoothie with a guy my age.

I hoped he would do the talking.

As I was leaving school, Zoe and Talia caught up to me and asked where I was going and I didn't think quickly enough to lie to them.

"Oh, cool, that's fun, let's go," Zoe said.

"No, I have to go alone."

"Why?" Talia asked with big eyes, ever searching for a drama.

"Because. Don't make me tell you."

"Tell us," she said in a hiss, looking around.

"I'm meeting someone. A boy."

She sucked in a breath. "The one from the cemetery?"

"Yes."

"Gothic."

Zoe said, "We won't make trouble. Let us come. We'll hide in the back."

"Please, you guys."

They frowned and pouted and finally relented. I watched them walk off and I felt bad and wanted to apologize but decided not to. I didn't feel sorry. I just felt a little more grown-up than I was accustomed to being. Telling the truth and all. Knowing they'd get over it. Not trying to make them happy so they'd like me. Was this what the rest of my life was going to look like? All these mature choices?

Thanks, Mom.

I walked into Larchmont village. I didn't pay attention to anyone. I just watched my shoes and tried to come up with an opening line. Maybe he wouldn't show. That would be a relief.

But he was there. Standing out front. Hands in his pockets. Pacing a little. Smiling when he saw me. Cuter than I remembered, and I wanted to run.

"Nice outfit" was his opening line.

I was in uniform, of course. That's what he was referring to. The short gray skirt and the white polo shirt and the sneakers and the blue hoodie.

"Great way to kick it off, ridiculing my look."

His smiled broadened. "It's not your look. And anyway, I mean it. It's sexy."

Well, that was good enough to shut me up, so I just stood there staring at him and here's what I eventually came up with:

"You didn't bring your drawing pad."

He shrugged. "I've already drawn you."

Now I was really stumped and feeling like I was either in love or being stalked.

"You drew me? That day?"

"It's more of a sketch. Does that weird you out?"

"A little."

"I just thought you were interesting."

"I prefer sexy."

He shook his head. "Pretty. That's the right word."

That actually made me blush and he saw it and we both laughed.

"I think it's time for a fruit drink," I said.

So I ordered a banana something and he ordered an orange-raspberry something and he paid and we sat down at a table.

We sucked on our straws for a minute and couldn't think of anything to say. The place was riddled with Hillsboro girls and some of them I knew and they spoke to me and raised their eyebrows in a question, gesturing with their heads toward Mick.

"I'm going to be the talk of the school on Monday," I said.

"Well, it's good to have a reputation."

"It is?"

"What's that Oscar Wilde quote? 'There is only one thing in the world worse than being talked about, and that is not being talked about.' "

I laughed. "You go around reading Oscar Wilde?"

"No, I go around reading quotes. It makes you sound smart."

We smiled at each other and sipped our drinks.

He said, "So tell me your story."

I looked at my banana concoction and had no idea where to begin.

"No, you first," I said.

So he told me his story. It was reasonably dramatic, the drug addict father who died alone in a hotel near San Francisco. And his mother, who worked as a nurse in a maternity ward. She was funny and smart, he said, and other than marrying her father, she had made good choices. She worked in the maternity ward because she loved babies. Looking at them reminded her of the resiliency of the human spirit (his words, or her words, not mine). She was often tired when she got home and they never seemed to have enough money, but they got by. They had a lot of friends in their apartment complex and sometimes they had block parties on the street where he lived in Westwood. His mother babysat on weekends to make extra money and he had a part-time job washing dishes at a restaurant. His goal was to get

168

into something called Risdee—Rhode Island School of Design, he explained—and eventually make it as either a fine artist or a graphic designer. He didn't care about getting married or having kids, but he figured that was because he was too young to think about it. He did want to fall in love, though, he said.

"What kind of guy are you?" I asked. "You actually say the 'l' word out loud and you tell girls they're pretty."

"Oh, I'm not normal. Did you think I was normal?"

"I guess not."

"Normal is too easy. Everybody does it."

He told me some more. He read books and he was going through a Kurt Vonnegut phase. His favorite subject in school, besides art, was math, and I made a face and he laughed. He loved music, all kinds, but his current favorites besides the Beatles (he said he didn't trust anyone who didn't like the Beatles so I quickly told him the John Lennon preschool story) were Green Day and Weezer and Queens of the Stone Age. He also loved the blues and soul music from the sixties. The Stax singles, he said, and Motown, and Phil Spector. I told him I loved all that music myself and it was my father who had turned me on to it.

"What about your mom?" he asked.

"She loved that music, too."

"But what did she turn you on to?"

It was hard to answer. He saw my expression change and he didn't fall for the fake smile I produced to cover.

He said, "I'm sorry. Bad topic."

"Yeah, stay away from the dead mother on the first juice date. That's definitely for a food or movie date."

He said, "I'll just let you bring it up when you're ready."

I said, "My mother wasn't who I thought she was."

"In a good way?"

"I don't know."

We were quiet for a moment. I sucked on my banana drink and it felt cold in my stomach.

"What about the Clash?" I asked him.

"Oh, yeah, possibly the greatest rock band of all time."

But the music portion of the discussion was over and the conversation just died. It got quiet. I knew it was time for my story and I knew I wasn't prepared to tell him.

I didn't want to keep it a secret, but it was too much. It was too big and I couldn't trust a stranger with it.

I felt a little of what my mother must have felt when she saw Noah the first time. She wanted to know him but was afraid she'd never get the chance. Because she was too damaged. She had too much history. She couldn't ask him to take it on.

I was a generation apart from the bad seed in my family. And Mick had a drug addict father so he ought to understand.

Still, I wasn't brave enough.

So I just told him the obvious, that I was a Hillsboro girl and my father was a lawyer and we were die-hard liberals. I took a chance and told him about how I wanted to cry in history class thinking about the Native Americans.

He said, "Aristotle said something to the effect that war will end when everyone is dead. It seems to be the natural state of things. Human nature."

"And that makes it okay?"

"Not okay," he said. "Human nature. People are dark."

I asked him if he believed in God and he said he believed in something but he wasn't sure what. I agreed.

He looked at me as if he were studying an exotic bird. I looked away from him and thought about my mother, refusing to look at my father in the parking lot. I understood what that was about. The eyes were too revealing.

I was afraid he was seeing the darkness in me. Not just the history but my own personal darkness. That was so new to me, I had no idea what it was or how deep it went.

It went deep enough to make me unsympathetic toward my father.

It went deep enough that I was afraid I'd never be able to care about my social life at Hillsboro again.

I had no idea who I was.

I didn't know if I'd risk my life for anything or anyone. I didn't know if I would turn someone in to the police or if I'd even care that they were breaking the law. I didn't feel anything strongly. I just wanted to fit in.

That was what the car had been about. Fitting in.

It wasn't about freedom or mobility or even maturity.

It was being part of the pack.

A car would have been a very different thing for my parents. If they had had some form of transportation, they could have run away together. And they needed to run away. They were stranded.

I just wanted to fit in.

How was that for a realization?

My mother was a genuine avenger. She risked her life to say the truth. My father had risked almost as much to help her. And I wanted to fit in.

I stared into my drink. I wanted Mick. I wanted him to be impressed with me. I wanted him to be my boyfriend and take me to movies. I wanted a picture of him on my dresser. I wanted us to hold hands and laugh like normal people.

But I was afraid to want it.

I only had a few minutes to come up with something worth admiring. Some character, some courage, some depth. Something that showed I had some nerve and creativity and a taste for adventure.

"Where do you think your mother is?" he asked me suddenly.

"I thought you weren't going to bring up the dead mother."

"I'm sorry. I panicked. There was a lull."

I smiled. "I don't know."

"Not in the graveyard, though."

"It used to be the only place that I felt her."

"Not anymore?"

I smiled and twisted the bird bracelet around on my wrist.

"Not anymore."

He smiled and looked at the bracelet but didn't ask.

"Where do you think your father is?"

He shrugged. "I never knew him well enough to wonder."

"Did he leave you anything? I mean, do you have his belongings? Did he write anything down?"

"Like a letter?" he asked.

"Yeah," I said quietly. "Like a letter."

"No, I wish he had."

"My mother wrote one. I read it."

It came out. Just like that. I wondered if the bananas in my smoothie were fermented, because I felt a little drunk.

"A letter to you?"

I shook my head. "It wasn't to me. But it was for me. In a way."

"What did she say in it?"

"A lot. It's complicated."

"I'd like to hear about it."

"I'd like to tell you. But not now."

He smiled. "That means I'm going to see you again."

"Yeah."

"So the juice date is going pretty well."

"Yeah," I agreed.

We stared at each other in a way that people my age are typically afraid to do. But he was different. I was different.

I wondered if my parents had stared at each other just this way.

I had always worried about dating—right up until this moment, in fact—because I knew my father wouldn't be able to tell me how to do it. He wouldn't be able to tell me how to recognize the right guy. He wouldn't like anyone I brought home. He might even forbid me to do it. He might say, "We're not like that," or "We're not from here," or "You're all I have."

So I tried to imagine what my mother would have said about dating and about Mick in particular.

I could almost hear her, but I knew it was really my own voice speaking for her.

Find someone special and don't settle. Find him and stay focused. Find more than one and learn what you have to learn and when you've learned enough, get married and stay that way.

I smiled suddenly because these sentences crossed a line where they didn't feel like mine anymore. Maybe she had always been talking to me. And I was learning how to listen.

What about Mick? I asked her.

I didn't hear anything except a loud sucking sound.

He had reached the bottom of his orange-raspberry drink. We both laughed at the awkwardness.

"Do people ever treat you weird?" he asked. "I mean, because of her."

"They did when I was little. Now it's like a status symbol."

"Why?"

"I don't know. It's strange at Hillsboro. We don't get to wear regular clothes and we don't have boys, so we find other things to be competitive about. Like grades and ancestors and strange history."

He laughed. "In public school, it's just the usual crap. Sneakers and iPods and you talked to my girl, I'll see you in the parking lot."

"And drugs, right? And people having sex in the bathrooms."

He laughed. "Yeah, just a bunch of losers with no plans for the future."

I felt my face turning red. "No, I didn't mean that."

"Sure you did. We know that's how you see us."

"Well, you think we're all spoiled and stupid."

He shook his head. "Just spoiled. But you're different."

I thought about it. "I wasn't all that different. Until recently."

"What changed?"

"That kind of falls in the dead-mother category."

"Oh," he said.

We looked into our empty drink cups.

"Want another?" he asked.

"No, thanks."

He glanced at his watch and said, "Is it over? I mean, the juice date."

I thought about it. I probably needed to get home. But I was worried I had not left enough of an impression on him. I hadn't proven I was more than a spoiled private school girl.

"The juice portion of the date might be over," I said. "But I want to take you somewhere."

"Where? Back to the cemetery?"

"No. Much better. But it depends on how game you are," I said.

"Oh, I'm game. I'm nothing but game."

"When do you have to be home?"

"Whenever I get there. Mom doesn't get back till ten tonight. She's got the late shift."

"Then I have an idea."

Because I did. It was a crazy idea, but sometimes the crazier the idea, the better.

That's what my mom would have told me.

It was time to have a backbone.

Maybe I was weird and superficial and confused, but the least I could do was have some courage. I could be brave. Like her.

• 2 •

We rode the bus down to Ocean Boulevard and took the long stairs down the Palisades bluff and the long bridge across Pacific Coast Highway. The sun was low over the water and the beach was empty.

The swell was big. I could tell that from the parking lot. The waves were at least twice as high as when Jen and I were out there. That scared me for a moment, but it was too late to lose my nerve. Besides, I figured, more room to stand up and ride. Weren't the big waves supposed to be good?

"The beach," Mick said. "Very romantic move. Are we getting in the water? Because it looks pretty cold."

"Watch this."

I grabbed his hand and led him over to a stand that rented boards and wet suits.

"I'll take that board there," I said, pointing. "What is that, an eight-point-oh? That'll do. And a wet suit."

The guy took my money and looked at Mick.

"How about you, dude?"

"I'm not actually a dude. I'm very land-based. I'll be a spectator."

"Are you sure?" I asked him. "Because I can teach you. I learned in a day."

"Not for beginners out there today," said the surfer dude.

"Yeah, I'll play it safe," Mick said. "But I want to see you."

"You know what you're doing, right?" the dude asked me.

"Yeah. Absolutely."

I had to change in the public bathroom because I hadn't been smart enough to bring a bathing suit. Well, smart didn't come into it. I was being impulsive and I wasn't used to living that way.

I stared into the mirror and my face was white with fear.

What the hell was I doing?

But the idea of getting into the water and standing on it made my stomach calm down. Mick was going to see the new me, the person I had every intention of being from now on. Not spoiled, not scared, someone who knew how to live, enough to make up for my mother and the red-haired girl down the well. I was going to make it count.

Mick said I looked hot in the wet suit and I just laughed and hoisted the board on my hip and chattered nervously as we walked toward the water.

"My dad says it's one of the true curiosities of Los Angeles that the community willingly turns the most valuable real estate over to the homeless. He says you'd never find people sleeping on the beach in Martha's Vineyard. Bag ladies or drug dealers in the Hamptons. That's not how it goes other places."

"It's good," Mick said. "The rich people are willing to share."

"My dad says it's because they are afraid of the sun."

"Yeah, probably. They're afraid of most things." Then he added, "Not you."

There were only a half dozen surfers out there. The good ones. The shortboarders. The guys who didn't put on a wet suit until January.

Jen was nowhere in sight.

In fact, there wasn't a girl in sight.

Except me. Standing there next to Mick, who might have been one of those afraid-of-the-beach people from the way he was responding to his surroundings.

We were in Santa Monica next to the pier, where the surf was usually on the small side, even if there was a swell in. But not today.

It was a shore break, which meant the waves formed and then delivered themselves directly onto the beach. Not like a point break, where the waves form far out in the water at an angle and are often slow and deliberate. A shore break is always harder because you have to paddle directly into the big white water, and the wave closes out faster, giving you less time to stand up. The advantage to the shore break was that the waves were smaller. But not today.

"Whoa," he said. "Are the waves always this big?"

"No. There's a swell."

"You're really going in?"

"I'll be fine," I told him, with no evidence to support it.

He stood there in his jeans and sneakers and his fatigue jacket, smiling.

The sun was starting its slow descent over the ocean. I knew I only had a few minutes to get this thing done.

While I was contemplating that, he stepped closer to me and leaned his head to one side. It looked like he was going to ask me a question but instead he put his lips right next to mine and I wasn't sure what he was doing and then I realized he was going to kiss me.

I jumped back as if I had been burned.

It wasn't graceful.

He straightened up and just stared at me. He blushed a little, but otherwise he was waiting for me to explain.

"I can't."

That was all I could say.

"Okay" was his response.

"It's not you, it's me."

"Okay. I just felt like doing that. I took a chance. It's really okay."

"I like you, Mick."

"But not like that. I get it."

"No, like that. Exactly like that. I just . . . can't."

He waited.

I had no idea what to say. Maybe I have a secret. Maybe I'm related to a criminal. Maybe my mother wasn't who I thought she was and I've never done a courageous thing in my life. Yet.

But I knew I couldn't let him kiss anyone but the person who was on the right path.

So I said, "I have to get in the water. I never kiss before that."

Which was technically true. It had never been an issue before. Now, suddenly, it was a policy.

"Later, then. Something to look forward to," he said.

"Right."

So I attached the leash to my leg and grabbed my board and ran into the waves and away from the only thing on earth that scared me more than kissing him.

Paddling out was a bitch, but I stayed on my board out of pure pride. A couple of times I had to turtle, which I really didn't know how to do, but I taught myself. For those of you wondering, turtling is when you actually flip over and turn upside down on your board as a wave breaks on you. Why would any sane person do that, you ask? We're not talking about sane people. We're talking about surfers. Surfers do it to keep from getting pummeled by the white water and to keep the board from flying out from under them and hitting another surfer. It's never cool to ditch your board, which is everyone's first instinct when they see a wall of crashing white water heading toward them. But it's a serious violation of surfer etiquette and fights have been known to break out. Jen had taught me all of this. I wasn't turtling out of any respect for my fellow surfers; I was doing it to impress Mick. But there were worse reasons to do things and certainly worse ways to learn.

After I had turtled a couple of times I felt brave. The real kind of courage that I was searching for, the kind that my mother had had and that I wanted to know more about. No, not the same kind. Just the beginning of it.

The waves were bigger than I could possibly explain and coming hard and fast. But I was determined. There was courage to be had out there in the water and I intended to take some home with me.

I got past the break zone and the water got a little bit flat between sets, but I could see the set forming in the distance.

Waves come in sets, you see. Most people don't know that, because they don't have to. Waves come in groups of six or seven. And it varies, the amount of time between sets. Because it was a big day, there wasn't much downtime between onslaughts.

I didn't have much room to get my wits about me. I straddled my board and saw Mick standing on the shore, watching. He looked smaller from this distance but just as cute, the way he had one foot on top of the other, the one hand shading his eyes and the other shoved in his pocket, and I imagined he was nervous on my behalf. I was going to show him. By God, when I was done, he was going to see something worth kissing. And my father would see someone who could rival my mother. And I would see it, too, and then I would be on my way.

I felt the wave before I saw it. I took one quick glance over my shoulder and it was on me and I started paddling faster than I ever had before. The wave lifted me up and I was high above the horizon and I was standing up before I knew it. I had this awesome moment of exhilaration and that sense of magic you get when it seems as if you're walking on water. I felt like I could do anything. I saw the shore moving toward me and I heard the roaring sound of the wave and I was all alone out there and I was the master of my universe. I was invincible. I had to reach for more.

So I started walking on my board. Like turtling, it was something I had never tried before. But I had seen Jen do it and I knew it was an advanced move. I took tiny steps at first and then got braver. I was getting close to the nose and I was thinking of Mick watching me, though I couldn't look at him, could only stare at the rails on my board, and I heard the sound of my breath pounding and competing with the roar of the wave. My heart was beating so hard I thought it might break through and I wanted to cry from the excitement and the triumph of it all.

And then it happened.

I don't know how it happened, just that it did.

I probably lost my footing. Or the wave turned or I turned. The nose of the board went down. I got all caught up in my success and forgot to stay in the moment. There are thousands of possibilities, but in hindsight, they don't matter. What matters is that I fell.

I fell hard. It took forever and it wasn't pretty. There was some flailing involved. My limbs felt like they didn't belong to me anymore, as if they might separate and go shooting off in all directions. I saw my board flying away from me and I was airborne and the ocean was waiting to swallow me whole. Even in that moment between the board and the water I was thinking about how it looked to Mick and I knew how it looked. It looked ridiculous. It looked like failure.

The ocean opened its mouth and sucked me in. I turned and tumbled like socks in a dryer and I couldn't tell up from down. I remembered Jen talking about this and some of that knowledge came back to me. The books said to relax and wait to be delivered. It said not to fight. So I didn't fight. I just tumbled. My head hit the sand and possibly a rock. I felt dizzy and I thought I might vomit or faint. I came up briefly and then another wave crashed on me and I went down again into the murky darkness and that's close to the last thing I remember.

The very last thing I remember, though, was everything getting still and I had a sense that it was all over one way or another. I was floating upside down and I could see the water and eventually the sky above me but I couldn't stand up. I couldn't because I was tied down to the bottom. I looked at my leg and saw that my leash was caught on a rock. I struggled to take my leash off but my fingers were weak and slippery and then I stopped trying and just stared at the watery sky and waited for the rest of my story.

· 3 ·

My mother looked exactly the way I remembered her. But she was clearer to me and I saw some things I had forgotten. That mole on her right temple, for example, and the way her forehead wrinkled when she raised her eyebrows at me. Her eyes were greener than anything I could think of. I would say greener than the ocean, but the ocean isn't really green except in poems. They were like rare gems, her eyes, the kind you see in jewelry stores under the case where it's too expensive to even ask. I couldn't stop staring into them.

She was sitting on the beach the way she used to do when she took me to watch the surfers. She was wearing jeans and a T-shirt and she was hugging her knees into her chest. Her hair was perfectly still and I remember thinking, there's always a breeze at the ocean, shouldn't her hair be blowing?

And if her hair isn't blowing, does that mean I'm dead?

And if I'm seeing her, that should certainly mean I'm dead.

But I wasn't afraid of being dead. I was just so happy to see her.

Then I saw myself. I was sitting next to her and I was wearing my wet suit and I wasn't the least bit wet. My hair was dry and it wasn't blowing either.

Then I was in my body, sitting next to her, but somehow still watching it from above. I was in both places at once.

She watched me for a moment.

"I'm not going anywhere," she said. "Look around."

I looked around. The beach was empty except for us. There was no Mick and there were no surfers in the water or strollers on the sand. No birds, even. But there were waves. They were falling softly on the shore, making very little noise, and I felt free and devoid of pain. I felt calm, too, like the whole big ordeal of being me was over.

And yet I was me. I was more me than I had ever been.

She said, "What was that about, Lynnie?"

"What do you mean?"

She gestured to the ocean.

"I wanted to surf. I wanted to show Mick." She waited for more and I tucked my head and said, "I wanted to be brave."

183

"Being brave isn't about being willing to die."

"I wasn't willing to die." I put my hands to my face and I could feel my skin but it felt different. "Am I dead?"

"Well, actually, there's no such thing. But that's not what we want to spend our time talking about, is it?"

I shook my head.

"I think you have a few questions for me," she said.

"Yeah."

"Go ahead."

I wanted to go ahead but I didn't know how.

She said, "Why don't I start?"

I nodded.

"You want to know how I hid my secret from you all that time. You want to know why. And you want to know how I ended up so content in my life after everything I had been through."

"Yes."

She laughed in that special way that she had. Her laugh sounded like music.

"Well, I could tell you but it wouldn't mean much. That is, I'm not the person to tell you."

"Who is?"

"I think you know."

"Daddy?"

"You have to let him in, Lynnie. You have to let him finish the job. Don't shut him out."

"But he's so hard to talk to."

"You make it hard."

"I do? How?"

"By hanging on to me. By making me the perfect one. I wasn't perfect."

"You seemed perfect."

"That's your memory. You've forgotten about all the times I sent you to your room for a time-out. Or about how I forgot to pick you up from school that day? You had to wait an hour in the principal's office and you didn't speak to me for a week. Then there was the time I forced you to eat your peas. And the countless times I yelled at you for making a mess. Your father defended you back then, don't you remember? She's just a kid, Cat, he said. Kids make a mess."

I tried hard to remember but I couldn't.

"I made you brush your hair when you didn't want to and I put dresses on you for fancy events and I once let you sleep in your bed after you had wet it just because I was too tired to deal with it."

I sucked in a breath. "You didn't do that."

She laughed. "No, I didn't. But I wanted to. I did a lot of things because I felt obligated and there were nights and weekends when I resented you because I wanted to go out somewhere and dance until the sun came up. The point is, I was human. And you've stopped letting me be that."

I opened my mouth to argue but nothing came out.

She said, "Meanwhile, your father has committed the sin of staying alive. Which means that he's continued to be human. And you can't forgive him for that. You can't even forgive yourself for the same thing."

"Yeah, well, I know I'm not perfect. I know I'm not even good."

She waved a dismissive hand at me. "Don't let that become your calling card. 'Not as good as my mother.' That's your whole thing now. It's boring."

I felt tears welling up and I suspected I wasn't dead, because surely there weren't tears after death. There weren't these feelings of sadness and regret in . . . I don't know, heaven, or wherever it is that you go. In this case, the beach in Santa Monica with nobody on it but us.

The tears came and then I was hyperventilating the way a three-year-old does and my words came out in choked sobs.

"Why did I have to find out about all that stuff? And why can't I let you be the way I remember?"

She said, "Because it's not the truth, Lynnie. And the truth is everything."

"Who were you?" I asked, overcoming my sobs. "You had this whole secret life."

"Not a secret life. A private life. Do you know the difference?"

I shook my head.

"Do you want to know?"

"I think so."

She looked at the ground and then at the sky as if she were waiting for guidance. I had a terrible feeling that she was going to disappear.

She said, "A secret life is what my father had. He couldn't exist in the world as he was. So he had to create something that no one knew about. It was a failure of nerve and a failure of confidence. It wasn't about private thoughts that he kept to himself. He started out with those but they became so powerful to him, he couldn't resist. He had to live in that power because his reality was so lacking. He couldn't speak his truth. He lived for the externals. He lived for his image. He only wanted to create an acceptable presence so he could go on indulging in his dark secrets. That's not the solution. Whatever is darkest in you needs to be dragged out into the light. Not ignored or denied. Acknowledged and announced. Then you can stop suffering. You weren't born to suffer."

"What was I born to do?"

She smiled. "Be yourself."

"I don't know how to do that."

"You started doing it when you met Mick and later when you heard the rest of my story. Your instinct toward honesty and courage was correct. But you got carried away. You wanted to be something you weren't. You wanted to know something before you had learned it. That's not the way."

"You saw Mick?" I asked.

"I see everything."

"Do you like him?"

She reached out for my hand and I could feel her skin, cool and smooth.

"I like him very much. I like the way he looks at you. He sees you. The real you."

"How can he see the real me when I don't?"

She laughed again. "Sometimes, most times, it takes someone outside of yourself to help you see who you are. They reflect it back to you. A good friend is like a mirror. They show you yourself. And you do the same for them."

"But who do you see?"

"I see my little girl. Bright and funny and furious and determined. But there are other things in you that I can't see.

"Because they are private."

She said, "Privacy is the world of things you know about yourself and don't need to share. It's your relationship with yourself. The way you cry at sad movies and sing in front of the mirror. The way you believe you'll be a movie star or win a Nobel Prize. Whatever it is. Those dreams you're entitled to. The difference is that you're not ashamed. Your private thoughts empower you. Secrets are something else. It's the part of yourself that you disown. Even to yourself. Then a strange kind of chemistry occurs and you start to love the secret and you think the secret is keeping you alive. I hope you'll never do that. I hope you'll want to take yourself and your private dreams and choose to be part of the dance."

I thought about that and I looked around the empty beach and I looked down at my wet suit, which was not wet or even sandy, and I was sure that I was dead.

"I don't think I'm going to get the chance to do anything again."

"Oh, yes, you will. If you want to."

"So death is a choice?" I asked, feeling angry out of nowhere.

"No, I didn't choose it. Not in a way you can understand. I had an appointment to keep. I was shown a scenario. A few scenarios. The ones where I stayed alive weren't as good as the one where I left."

"You're really going to have to explain that."

"I can't, Lynnie. One day you'll understand, but not soon."

She was still holding my hand and I could feel her skin and I had no idea where I was or what was going to happen next.

"I don't know what to do," I said.

"You'll know when it's time to know."

I suddenly felt restless and jittery. All of my senses came

back to me, and the sand was scratchy. The wind was whipping up and my hair was blowing around even though my mother's stayed perfectly still.

"I don't feel so good," I said.

My mother nodded. "I know."

"Everything hurts."

"It hurts because you feel it. Because you're alive. Make the most of it."

"Wait, don't leave."

I could feel my body and it felt heavy. Everything was cold. I had a headache. Something itched and there were sounds I couldn't identify springing up around me.

She stood up, turned, and started walking down the beach. I tried to stand up but I couldn't. My limbs felt as if they were filled with wet sand and all my nerve endings were exposed. The pain was rushing in like the white water, coming toward me at eye level, and there was no escape. I tried to say something. My voice crackled and popped like a voice on the end of a cell phone that was losing its connection. The sky suddenly got very low and the sun was hot and everything ached.

"She's waking up," I heard someone say. "We've got her back."

I opened my eyes and I wasn't on the beach at all. I was in some kind of room with machinery all around me. People were dressed in green and someone was holding a mask over my face and I wanted to stand up and scream. But everything hurt and the light from somewhere stung my eyes.

I saw my father bending over me. He was wearing a shirt and tie but the shirt was soaked with sweat and his face was all wrenched with worry and there were tears.

He leaned over me and grabbed my hand.

I felt it.

It was sweaty and warm, not like my mother's hand at all.

"Lynnie," he said. "Lynnie, come back."

I'm back, I heard myself saying. But I wasn't talking because the mask was over my mouth.

I stared into his eyes until I really saw him. He was my father. I looked like him. I had always looked like him. And I wanted to get to know him.

I squeezed his hand and he smiled and laid his head against my chest.

I closed my eyes and trusted I would know what to say when the time came.

And I knew the time was coming so I slept.

SIXTEEN
and I've Stopped Counting

• 1 •

So much for that nice moment.

When I woke up in the hospital my father was angry.

He started yelling around the time I noticed that I was hooked up to machines and there was a bag dripping some kind of disgusting gunk into my arm.

"What's this?" I asked.

"What's what?" he responded, jerking awake in his chair. He had been dozing off, his head rolling to the side.

"This thing in my arm?"

"It's an IV. It's been keeping you alive. Something you seemed to have lost interest in yourself."

"Okay, wow. Happy to see you, too."

"Did you really think I wasn't going to have something to say about this?"

"I thought you might wait until I was out of the hospital gown."

"Yeah, well, I thought you might not make it out of the hospital gown."

A nurse came in just as our voices were rising.

"Oh, good," she said with fake cheerfulness. "Miss Lynne is finally making sense."

"When wasn't I making sense?"

"For the last two days," my father informed me.

"I've been here two days?"

"Two and a half," the nurse said gleefully. "Now, let's look at those stats."

She took my blood pressure and stuck a thermometer in my ear and said everything was fine.

"This might be your first day of solid food," she said, as if I were about to get a glimpse of my first porn video. She winked at me and went out.

"What wasn't I making sense about?" I asked my father, who was standing now, breathing hard through his nose and looking at me the way he did when I hid a grade from him or lied about something.

"You were babbling, Lynne. You had a head injury. You weren't making sense and, frankly, nobody was sure if you ever would."

I took a breath and looked at my lap, at the oatmeal-colored blanket with fur balls on it. I wondered about all the other sick people who'd gotten covered up by it and it grossed me out. The whole hospital thing was grossing me out, and it wasn't helping that my dad was yelling and glaring.

"Was I talking about Mom?" I asked.

He raised his chin. "As a matter of fact you were."

I didn't feel it was the time to say, That's because I saw her. So I just kept quiet.

I remembered it, though. All of it. And that was why the

hospital room wasn't scaring me so much. I knew I wasn't going to die. It surprised me that my father ever thought I was going to. I tried to see it from his point of view but, as usual, failed.

I looked at my nightstand and saw some balloons from Zoe and Talia. There was a card with a wave on it. I opened it and it said, "Lizard, the big swell, by yourself? You're an ass. Get well. Jen."

I had a sudden recollection and looked around the room.

"Where's Mick?"

My father moved toward the bed, his hands on his hips.

"Who?"

"Mick. The guy I was with."

He shook his head and for the first time I was a little scared. Had I imagined Mick, too? Or had he died trying to save me? Or had he just deserted me on the beach and left me to my demise?

So much for my first date.

"Mick," my father repeated. "He introduced himself as Michael."

I smiled. "He was trying to impress you."

"He didn't. You can imagine how he didn't."

"What? Why are you mad at him?"

"I don't know him, Lynne. I'd never seen him before. I didn't know anything until the cops called me, and then I was standing on the beach while the paramedics were pumping water out of your lungs and there was some kid with long hair and an army jacket standing nearby, pacing and saying he knew you, and imagine how I felt. I knew less than anybody on that beach about what was going on."

Try to picture a man who is always in control of himself, a lawyer, no less, used to making arguments in front of a bunch of strangers where somebody's life is on the line . . . picture that guy waving his hands around and yelling at a teenager hooked up to an IV in a hospital bed under a ratty blanket.

And then picture yourself with a terrible headache and a lingering vision of your dead mother and your five-minute boyfriend and your grandfather the murderer and you might get a mild notion of how I felt.

Try not to get yourself into this predicament.

But I was in it and I didn't know what to do. I wanted my father to calm down. I wanted to see my mother again. I wanted to tell someone who would understand. I wanted to see Mick again but now I wasn't sure I ever would.

"Were you mean to him?" I asked.

"To who?"

"Mick?"

"I wasn't mean to him. I just sent him home."

"That was mean."

"I don't know him, Lynnie. I don't know how you know him. I don't know what you're doing half the time. I don't know who you are anymore."

"Isn't that why you gave me the letter? To tell me who I am?"

This stopped him cold. I knew it wasn't fair, but I was tired of him yelling.

I could see in his eyes a split second of relief that I had that kind of recall. If I could remember the letter then I wasn't so far gone.

He stared at me and for the first time I saw that his eyes were watery and I felt shocked at myself and at him.

"So you do remember," he said.

"Yes, I remember. I'm not brain damaged."

"Is that why you pulled this stunt? Because of the letter?"

"I don't know. I haven't had time to process it."

"And what about the boy? How does he fit in?"

"He's nice. We had a juice date. He lives in Westwood."

"How did you meet him?"

"In the cemetery, talking to Mom. He was drawing. He's an artist."

"It would have been nice if you had told me."

"It would have been nice if you were the kind of person I could tell."

He wiped at his eyes and I felt even worse than before.

"No, I take that back," I said.

This caught him off guard. He'd never known me to take anything back. I'd never known myself to, either.

"I didn't go down there to hurt you. I went to show off for Mick. And for myself. I wanted to be brave."

"Brave?" he said as if the word shocked him.

"Yes, like her."

"But you don't need to be brave, Lynnie. She was brave so you wouldn't have to be."

"What does that mean?"

"She fought through all that so you could have a good life. So you wouldn't have to worry. This is her history, not yours."

"How does that work? Her history stops with me?"

"Of course it doesn't. She saw her own story ending and she wanted to start another one. God, why are we even talking about this? You nearly died."

"Because I nearly died. That's why."

I considered, for a second, telling him about seeing Mom on the beach. But I knew it wouldn't help. I knew it was destined to be my private life. And I remembered the difference. A private life is just for you. A secret life involves others.

My father said, "People have things to overcome. People make sacrifices for each other. For the future. For the sake of their character. That's what I wanted you to get from it all. People do what's necessary."

I couldn't listen anymore. I was laughing. Now he really was looking at me as if I had lost my grip on reality. But I wasn't the one yelling at an intensive care patient, now was I?

"What?" he demanded.

"This all started with a car. I wish I'd never mentioned it. And the funny thing is, I don't even have my license yet."

He looked at me for a long time. "You don't?"

I shook my head.

"Why not?"

"You have to have a car to get a license."

"I could have taken you."

"You didn't. Is this really the time, Dad?"

This actually made him smile. He sat down on the bed. He shook his head, smiling at nothing, and then he put his arms around me and swayed me back and forth with my IV bag swinging and the sudden motion causing a machine to start bleeping and I could feel him crying against my shoulder even though he wasn't making any noise.

I stopped myself from crying, too. Honestly, one wrecked person was enough for the moment.

• 2 •

"You're wondering how she got to California."

My father talking. Me in and out of a drug-induced haze. Days disappearing into said drug-induced haze.

We were in my hospital room. It was the third day of my recovery. Everything I owned hurt and every time they started talking about letting me leave, I would throw something up or faint during one of my expeditions down the hall.

I was getting frustrated and my father was starting to look a little bit old. At least to me. Not to the doctor who came by to check on me every afternoon, one Dr. Penny Torgensen of Norwegian descent, a graduate of USC medical school, originally from Minnesota, who lived alone in Venice with her cat and her African gray parrot. She managed to relay all that information to my dad within five seconds of knowing him and he managed to forget it all in the same amount of time. She looked like an *American Idol* first-rounder, the one they drop because she's too good and too smart, and when she saw my dad her whole expression changed and she got a bit giggly. He couldn't even see it. I liked that about her, and if I were feeling stronger I would have helped the whole process along, but it was pretty much all I could do to stare at crossword puzzles and write down a three-letter word every half hour.

The other thing about Dr. Penny Torgensen was that she was a surfer and she explained to my dad that this shouldn't scare him off the sport for life. It was a freak accident, it almost never happened, I shouldn't have been in that swell, but I'd know

197

better next time. Wouldn't I, she asked me, giving me what I supposed was the universal surfer's wink.

I would know better next time. I could hardly think of surfing again. All I could think of was my mother's letter and her subsequent visitation and my dark history and my five-minute boyfriend and my head pounding like someone was squeezing it in a doorjamb.

Dad said, "I learned about it later. When I ran into her. In Westwood."

"Learned what? Why are we in Westwood?"

"About how she got to California. Your mother."

"Oh."

"You never asked me that."

"I figured she took a bus."

"Several buses."

"Did you know she was there? I mean, when you went to law school at UCLA?"

"No. It was one of those things that makes you believe in . . . I don't know. Something bigger."

I settled back on my pillow and he pulled his chair closer. I was in a mood to listen. The drugs were settling me into a calm, sleepy place. It was like hearing a bedtime story.

He was a student at UCLA law school. He wandered into the village one day for a coffee at the local coffee shop. She was the one who waited on him. He didn't recognize her at first. Her hair was shorter and she looked older. Plus she was wearing some goofy uniform. They talked about his order for a long moment before their eyes connected. He said she looked away as if she didn't want to be recognized and he said, "Cat? Catherine Pittman, is that you?"

She denied that it was her. She said her name was Lucy. He decided to let it drop and he took his coffee drink from her and went out onto the patio to drink it. But then she followed him out and said, "How did you know me?"

And he said to her, which you have to admit was a pretty great line, "How could I forget you?"

At least that's what he said he said. Maybe he came up with it later. It made a good story. But I decided just to go with it.

I asked him what happened next.

He said, "I took her for a walk. I talked her into taking a break from her coffee bar job. I was always talking your mother into things. Breaking the rules, mostly. As you can imagine, she never wanted to break the rules. Daughter of a criminal and all. She was big on law and order. She was big on truth."

"I remember this part. She was all about truth."

So, he told me, they went walking, and she explained what had happened to her since that day at the police station. Her father had taken her home, hadn't said much to her that night. He let her walk around for days, suffering, wondering when the other shoe was going to drop. When he dropped it, it was in a subtle but powerful way. He took her out of school one day without warning and drove her to the next town over to meet with a psychologist. Mom said the whole experience was underwhelming. She just did some tests and answered a few questions and they shone a light in her eyes and tested her hearing and that was that.

Later he gathered the family together and announced, in front of her, that Catherine had had a nervous breakdown. The doctor had concluded that she had had a temporary but profound break with reality. If her stress levels were kept to a minimum and her social engagements were limited, she should soon return to normal. In the meantime, everyone should consider her fragile mental state before investing in anything she had to say.

The whole family was there, Mom told him. Her brother Gregory, Suzanne, her sister Sandra, her own mother who, she said, listened to the whole thing with a low level of interest, as if her ability to get all worked up about her children had been used up, like energy leaking out of a battery. By then she was crazy in denial. She smoked and drank iced tea and stared out the window.

Her siblings looked at her with a mixture of sympathy and suspicion. She knew it was all over. There was no one to turn to. She only had to endure her time at home.

It was devastating, she told him, being called the crazy one when you know you're the only one with a direct link to anything resembling reality.

"How did she survive it?" I asked.

"I can only tell you what she told me. That it had to do with me. The fact that I believed her. And she knew I believed her. That helped her stay sane."

"But you didn't talk to her again?"

"She wouldn't let me."

"Why?"

"She wanted to keep me out of it. She didn't want to drag me into it."

"But you should have insisted."

He nodded as if he had turned that very thing over in his brain for most of his life. And I felt bad because I knew I had hit a nerve and I knew it was easy for me to say.

"I was sixteen, Lynnie. That's all I have to say in my defense."

That summer she had taken her life savings and her father's silver coin collection and she had bought a bus ticket to the West Coast. She felt guilty about the coin collection, Dad told me. She actually wanted to pay her father back for it. Dad, the lawyer, gently explained that stealing silver from a murderer wasn't going to be her undoing. It was a matter of survival.

She made it to California on the bus and she found work and Dad didn't ask what kind. I knew she had cleaned houses because she told me once when I was little. I was watching her move like a lightning bolt with a sponge through the bathroom and I asked her how she knew how to do that so well and she told me.

But this was how she said it: "Oh, I did it to make a little extra money when I was in college."

Was she ever in college? I asked my dad.

Later, he said. After they got married. She studied philosophy and literature. She wanted to be a writer.

Did she ever write anything?

He looked off when I asked. It made him smile.

"She wrote poems. I read them. Then she burned them. I wish she hadn't."

"Why'd she burn them?"

"She was afraid they weren't good."

"Were they?"

He nodded.

He waited a minute and said, "She wanted to burn the letter, too. She was surprised to find I'd kept it all that time."

"But you didn't let her."

201

"I thought it was important. It was history."

Finally he looked at me and smiled.

He said, "She was happy, you know. She made it."

"Did he look for her?" I asked. "Her father. When she left."

Dad shook his head. "He didn't want to find her. He wanted her to disappear."

"And he never got caught."

"No. He died."

"And the rest of the family?"

"Her mom died, too, we heard. Everyone else is somewhere in the South. There were camps. Everyone was against her. She didn't feel she needed to look back."

"So that's the story. Bad guy gets away with it. Good girl run out of town. Fairy-tale marriage. Dead in a car wreck. Father and daughter left behind to misunderstand each other. I'm looking for the justice."

"Don't get obsessed with that."

"Then I'm looking for the point."

"They lived out their stories. All of them. It's what we're here to do. How do you want your story to go? That's the point I was trying to make. It's not about what happens when we die. It's about what happens when we live. It's about creating character because that's what we take with us and it's what we leave behind."

"She had character."

He nodded.

"I want to have character, too," I told him.

"You're well on your way."

"Because of her."

He shook his head. "Because of you. The choices you have made."

"To surf in a big swell."

He smiled. "It was the wrong thing to do. But it was for an admirable reason."

"Yeah, I get that now."

"Character comes from doing the right thing. You listen to yourself. You have an instinct and you don't ignore it. As much as possible, you send fear packing."

I nodded. "From the guy who won't go on a date or let me drive a car."

"I'm working on it."

"Or ask out the doctor."

He stared at me for what seemed like a long time. "I thought I was imagining that."

"Please. Do something before I get embarrassed."

"What if she says no?"

"Character's a bitch, isn't it?"

He smiled. "You're babbling again."

"I'm on drugs," I said, and closed my eyes.

· 3 ·

December 22

Dear Mick,

Thank you for your letter, which I got right before I left town. I was out of it for a while. They wouldn't let me take calls at the hospital and my father carried that tradition over when I finally got home. I've told you how overprotective he is. He claims he's getting better. But you might as well know, he blamed you for the whole surfing incident, which is just ridiculous.

Well, that's not entirely true. He blamed you for half of it and me for the other half. He wasn't happy. To be fair, I nearly died and all. That didn't sit well with him. And I was being an idiot. I apologize for the whole ordeal. I was showing off for you. I wanted you to think I was superfabulous, an international woman of mystery. But now that I'm coming clean about everything, I'll admit that was my second time surfing in the whole history of being me.

It won't be the last, though. I figure once you nearly die doing something, you're protected under the lightning-doesn't-strike-twice law. Maybe I can get you to try it. Presuming you're remotely interested and want to go anywhere near a large body of water with me.

I would love to take you up on your suggestion that we should move on to a food date, but that won't happen until after New Year's. I'm out of town. I'm sorry I didn't get a chance to call and tell you that. But the fact is, the reason I'm out of town over the Christmas holiday is a complicated one and I want to share it with you in person. As it is, I can give you a few details.

I'm in a place called Union Grade. My mother and father grew up here. They met in high school and again after college. While they lived here, they both knew about a terrible crime that was committed and they tried to tell the police but no one believed them.

The crime happened to a girl my age named Jackie. In fact, I was named after her. She was my father's cousin. My mother saw it happen.

It was her father who killed the girl.

Oh, look, apparently I'm telling you the whole story now.

I was afraid to tell you. I was afraid of how it would sound. But now that I'm writing it, it doesn't have such a terrible feel to it. It just feels like the truth, and as someone once told me, the truth just is. There's no other quality to it, like good or bad or right or wrong.

My mother tried to teach me the difference between secret and private. This is not a secret anymore. It's been told. When it was a secret, it enslaved a lot of people. Once it was told, it set a lot of people free, even though it caused pain. And I guess that's how it works.

So I'm not telling you a secret. But I am telling you something private. I hope you understand what that means. I trust you. And after trust, who knows? Maybe fun, maybe frolic, maybe scandal.

I make jokes to cover up my insecurity. I didn't invent that process. Bear with me.

I like you and I have since I first saw you and I hope you feel the same way.

But back to Union Grade, Virginia. My dad and I flew to Washington, did the whole twelve-monuments-in-a-day routine, then drove four hours down to this town, which is far from anything you'd ever want to know about, practically in North Carolina, which is a state the guidance counselors in L.A. don't even mention when going over colleges.

I was all prepared to be a snob and hate it, but the truth is, it's beautiful. I'm not really a writer, not like my mother was, so I won't do a great job of describing it. It's the mountains, really, and the trees. Everywhere you turn, some green hillside or blue mountain peak or a vast network of evergreens. There are all kinds of trees—right now a lot of them are naked but still beautiful, with their branches reaching out like arteries, bending in the wind and just waiting for the leaves to return to them.

Dad says that in the fall, it's magical, when all the foliage turns to red and orange. He's talking to me a lot more than he used to. He's all excited to be here and when he remembers things his eyes get a glow and it's like I can see the guy who was once happy, before he got his heart broken, before he decided that his role in life was to be a bereft widower.

That's changing, I think. He's walked away from me a couple of times to indulge in a private cell phone call to one Dr. Penny Torgensen. She took care of me in the hospital and did everything but a belly dance to impress him. He finally noticed.

Anyway, there's something about this place. The quality of the light. The clouds. The ground, which is red in a lot of places instead of brown. Red clay, they call it, and in the summer, my father says, it's red dust. But it's a valuable commodity because it's what they use to make brick. He finds it amusing that everyone spends a fortune to import brick in Los Angeles. Back East, it's considered the cheapest building material. None of the rich people have redbrick houses. They prefer wood or quarry stone. Dad says it's the same way people in L.A. don't appreciate the ocean. Anything that's right up under you doesn't seem special.

I've never identified with any place except California, but I can imagine myself belonging to this part of the earth. I can imagine that the trees or the red clay would speak to me. I can imagine growing up here and making friends and dreaming about the world as my mother did. I can imagine longing to get out, too. Part of why I like being here is that I know we can leave.

He showed me the house he grew up in. It wasn't as horrible as he remembered. I thought it was kind of nice, even. It looked like pictures you've seen of early American houses in New England or Williamsburg, but it wasn't old and it was kind of pretentious. Someone had cut down a large oak tree he remembered being right outside his bedroom window, and that made him angry. He has this thing about not destroying nature. I suggested that lightning might have struck it and he didn't dismiss the idea. He allowed it to cheer him up. He said,

"That happens here, you know. We had real honest-to-God thunderstorms. Not what passes for weather in Los Angeles."

Then he showed me my mother's house. It was an actual Victorian house, built right after the Civil War, but someone had put ugly yellow siding on it and painted the windowsills forest green. It had a wraparound porch with rockers and a swing and an antique milk can by the door. It had columns (Doric—those are the plain ones, right?) and someone had stuck an American flag on one of them, and Dad found that amusing and distasteful—from an aesthetic rather than a political point of view.

He showed me the high school, which was your basic ugly 1970s L-shaped architecture (that's how he described it), which could have doubled as a detention center. We stood and looked at the track field where he used to run and then we stood and looked at the tennis courts where my mother played, and finally at the parking lot where he used to meet her after school. He didn't get as weepy as I'd imagined. He even smiled.

When we were standing in the parking lot, his cell phone went off and it was Dr. Penny again, and he took the call and chatted with her. I thought that was a good sign. He didn't consider it hallowed ground anymore. It was just a place from his past.

Finally he took me to the spot. The place where it all really happened.

I was nervous to go there and I was sure he was, too. We drove to the end of this long row of houses that were surrounded by woods. At the beginning of the road, the houses were new and expensive-looking with nicely kept yards, all full of flowers and hedges and fancy lawn furniture. But as it got closer to the end, toward the woods, the houses got smaller and the lawns were full of toys and cheap plastic chairs and tacky gnomes.

I said to my father, "Wouldn't the rich people want to live near the woods?"

He said, "They're afraid."

"Why?"

"Because it's always been the poor part of town out here. And they don't know how to change that. Plus, it's like the ocean in L.A. They're afraid of what might be in the woods."

"What might be in there? You mean animals?"

"Animals," he said. "Monsters. Fairies. Dragons."

"Seriously, Dad."

"I'm speaking symbolically. Anyway, they aren't entirely wrong, are they?"

"I guess not."

"The woods are unsupervised. Unmonitored. They don't account to anyone. Even now. That was the problem with the whole place when we were growing up. The town was too remote. It wasn't accountable to anyone. It's better to be accountable. That's the whole plan behind society. We answer to each other. Coexistence. Consideration."

He stopped talking as we actually stepped into the woods. It was quiet in there. Nothing moved because it was winter and there were no animals around. A few birds darted about, just as my mother described in her letter. But other than that, nothing but the sound of the wind moving across the carpet of dried leaves. And then the smell of the evergreens. The cedars, mostly, and pines. There were so many of them, nothing like the landscape in California. It smelled like a huge Christmas tree lot, only stronger, and I saw the branches and the needles swaying in the wind, and I thought of my mother wandering through the woods and calling for her father.

My own father was holding my hand very tight. Every snap of a twig made him hold it tighter. I thought he might cry but he didn't. He just kept walking and I kept letting him lead me.

Once I looked behind me to picture her running away, back to the truck. I couldn't see our car anymore. I wondered what it would feel like to be chased and I couldn't imagine it. Didn't want to imagine it.

Finally my father stopped and stood very still and looked at the sky. I did the same. There was nothing in it but a few cirrus clouds. It was a bright winter blue. And it was pleasant to stare at it. It looked like a way out. It looked like a painting that everyone had the privilege to see. And when I looked up, I knew it was possible you were staring up, too, somewhere three thousand miles away, and that even though the sky might look different to you, it was the same sky, the same sun, and we were connected under all this.

That was how she must have felt, staring up. Connected to someone she hadn't even met, and to a world of people she longed to join, and maybe every time she looked up, she found the courage to believe in that.

My father put his arm around my shoulders. He said, "I'm glad we came back. It was so much darker in my mind."

"Yeah, it's really just woods."

He nodded. "I don't know why I thought it would be more."

But I know why.

It's all about perspective, Jen explained. When you're lying on your stomach paddling into a wave, it looks enormous because you're at eye level. But when you jump off your board and stand up, you can see how small it is and it brushes right by you.

My father and I have both been paddling into the past at eye level. We just had to stand up to it.

Yours,
Lynne

SEVENTEEN

Mick closed the book and looked at me.

We were standing in the parking lot at Santa Monica beach, near the location where I had once almost died. It was night and the light from the bonfire on the beach was spilling across the sand and landing on us. It made him look tanned and exotic. His hair was still long and he still pushed it away from his face when he was nervous. The book made him a little nervous but it also made him smile.

There was music coming from the bonfire, too. Old stuff. Classic rock. People were getting sentimental. Bonfires weren't usually allowed on the beaches of Santa Monica, but this was the one night of the year when the cops made exceptions.

"What do you think?" I asked.

He said, "I think it was a lot of work."

"Not that much. Typing, cutting, pasting."

"A lot of typing, though."

I shrugged. "Good practice for a future reporter."

"That's not what you said in the journal. You claim you're not a good writer."

"Not poetic. Not good at making things up. Somewhat better at telling the truth."

He smiled. "I think you'll be great at it."

"And you'll be a famous artist. And we'll meet in New York and go to galas."

"I don't see how that's going to happen. I'll be stuck in Rhode Island without a car."

"Take the train. When you get to New York, you won't need a car."

"Do they allow scholarship students on the grounds of NYU?"

"There aren't any grounds. It's just the city. Everybody's welcome. Even people without cars. Why do you think I picked it?"

"You know what I mean."

"Stop doing the Romeo-and-Juliet thing. I'm over it."

He smiled, rubbing his fingers across the cover.

"I'm flattered," he said. "That you'd do this."

"I want you to remember me."

"Yeah. But this makes me feel like you think I won't. Or that it's somehow the end."

"If the story of my life proves anything, it's that nothing ends. Look at my parents. Look what they overcame. Look how chance helped them out."

"You don't believe in chance."

I smiled. I bumped his knee with mine. "God, then. But artists don't believe in that."

"Some do," he said.

211

"Hey, you guys, get over here and socialize. No isolating. This is a bonding experience!"

This was Talia's voice drifting across the sand. She and Zoe were waving to me. They were talking to two guys I didn't recognize. Friends of Mick's. He had introduced them and obviously they were having no trouble throwing away the boundaries between private and public school.

This was the night where all the kids came together. Graduation night. The same for us as it was for most of the public schools. And everyone got together on the beach for the bonfires. People met and mingled and got to know each other as equals, just for a while, before flying off to parts unknown. We were scattering like marbles. But tonight, on the beach, we were all the same.

He smiled and took my hand and brushed it against his lips. He said, "I didn't really wear an army jacket, did I?"

"Oh, yes, my friend. The journal doesn't lie."

"What's your excuse? You were interested in a guy in an army jacket."

"I saw past it."

"Really, now. And why didn't you ever mail that letter to me? The one you wrote in Union Grade?"

"Because I ended up telling you everything on the phone. And I was afraid you would think it was sentimental and girlish."

"What changed your mind?"

"I'm older."

"By a year."

We laughed.

"I trust the way you feel about me," I said.

He touched the book a little bit longer, then handed it back to me.

"I can't take it, Lynnie."

"What do you mean?"

"It's everything that matters to you. It's your mother's letter and it's the journal you kept all that time and it's your past. I can't take it."

"It's not my past. It's just a recording of it."

"But your mother's letter. What if something ever happened to it?"

"I had some Benedictine monks write it out on a scroll for me. It's copied and saved and on a disk. Information age, remember? Saving the letter itself is just sentimental. And I'm not."

He smiled. "This gesture isn't sentimental?"

"No, it's romantic. Do I have to give a semantics lesson? Anyway, my dad even understood that we had to get rid of it. He tried to burn it after we got back from the trip."

I remembered that moment, coming down in the middle of the night, finding him sitting in front of the fire with the manuscript on his lap. He wasn't sad or scared or anything. He just believed that the trip home had given him closure and he wanted to move on to the next stage of his life. I didn't disagree. But I felt the letter was mine to burn. Or save. I hadn't decided in that moment what to do.

But not long after Mick and I started dating, I knew what I had to do. Stuck in my drawer, it remained a secret, and the point of a secret was to expose it and pass it along. Giving it to Mick meant that it would go out into the world and find its own purpose. And the point, the ritual, the ceremony of giving him all this was to let him know that I intended to remember. As long as you remember who you are, what matters to you, who the players are in that drama, then the future is nothing but possibility. It's when you forget who you are that it all turns to pain. Remember, but don't get stuck. Remember and pass it on.

"I can't believe he wants you to give it to me," Mick said. "He's never been my biggest fan."

"He likes you now."

"He tolerates me."

"No, it's moved into like. Because of Penny. Stepmothers have that kind of effect. The good ones, anyway. She argues the feminine perspective."

He laughed. "Remind me to send her a thank-you note."

"Just take the book," I said. "It's yours."

"What if I lose it?"

"It's yours. Do whatever you want with it."

"But honestly, I'll be so paranoid about losing it."

"It's just a book. And the thing you're really worried about losing, you can't."

He looked at me. "I can't lose you? Even in New York City?"

"You can't lose this," I said, touching his face. "What we are right now in the moment."

"And after the summer?"

"That will take care of itself."

"Seriously, you two! The party is not in the parking lot! Stop lusting after cars, Lizard, it's not gonna happen." This was Jen, my surfing buddy, using my surfing nickname.

"I'm gonna miss that one," I said.

"Where's she going?"

"University of Hawaii. You have to ask?"

"I guess we all end up in the right place," he said.

He touched the birds dangling around my wrist.

"You're not giving me this?"

"No, the birds stay with me."

I heard the music drifting from the beach and I put my arms around his neck and he pulled me in close. It was an old song, something my mother might have listened to with Noah, sitting in the parking lot after tennis, staring at the sky and daring to imagine a future.

Me, I didn't have the same kind of battle to fight.

I was already in the dance. All I had to do was move.

BARBARA HALL is the author of seven novels and has written and produced numerous television shows, including *Northern Exposure, Chicago Hope,* and *Judging Amy.* She created the Emmy-nominated series *Joan of Arcadia.* She also writes and performs music with her band, the Enablers. Her music has been featured on several network television shows and is available at Handsome-Music.com. Barbara Hall lives in Santa Monica, California, with her daughter, Faith.